POSSESSION

by

REESE GABRIEL

CHIMERA

Possessing Allura first published in 2005 by
Chimera Publishing Ltd
PO Box 152
Waterlooville
Hants
PO8 9FS

Printed and bound in Great Britain by
Cox & Wyman, Reading.

This book is sold subject to the condition that it shall not, by way of trade or otherwise, be lent, resold, hired out or otherwise circulated without the publisher's prior written consent in any form of binding or cover other than that in which it is published, and without a similar condition being imposed on the subsequent purchaser.

The characters and situations in this book are entirely imaginary and bear no relation to any real person or actual happening.

Copyright © Reese Gabriel

The right of Reese Gabriel to be identified as author of this book has been asserted in accordance with section 77 and 78 of the Copyrights Designs and Patents Act 1988

POSSESSING ALLURA

Reese Gabriel

This novel is fiction – in real life practice safe sex

'This whip is made for use on animals,' he informed her, somewhat unnecessarily. 'Are you an animal, slut?'

Allura feared a trick question. 'I-I don't know, master.'

'Then I shall have to educate you, shall I not?' he drawled, brushing the leather coils over her treacherously hard nipples. 'A whip like this doesn't just punish a female,' he went on, Allura barely hearing his goading ramblings, 'it fucks her.'

Allura accepted the handle pressed to her lips, and without being told she parted them and he pushed it deep, her jaw aching as her mouth filled with pungent leather. Frightening herself with her obedience she sucked, wanting the feel of it all the way to the back of her throat, the smell and taste of leather filling her nostrils and her mouth, mingling sickeningly with the dungeon keeper's odor and the stench of the foreboding dungeon, and the constant pull of the cuffs on her wrists, pulling her body so vulnerably taut as she hung there.

'How about it?' He removed the saliva coated handle from between her lips. 'Ready to be whipped?'

Chapter One

The slave girl gasped in horror as the hairbrush slipped from her fingers to the floor at her mistress' feet. The count stood at nine hundred and ninety-one strokes to the princess' golden locks – so close to her quota of a thousand, and yet so far.

'Forgive your slave, mistress.' She fell to her knees, putting her forehead to the marble floor. 'Veeta begs to be allowed to begin again.'

The Princess Allura shook out her long sandy tresses and smiled, cat-like. 'Too late, my inattentive little slut.'

'Mercy,' pleaded the barefoot girl as she lowered herself to her belly in the pitifully short rag of a covering, more a provocation to indulge than an actual garment.

Allura beheld the girl's trembling, prostrate form through cold eyes, feeling as always the special thrill that came with having total control over a fellow female. 'I grow weary of your sloppiness, Veeta, and your disobedience. Have you any reason to offer why I should not have you put to death this time?'

'No, mistress, I have none,' she replied piteously.

The fact that the slave had been denied sleep twenty-four hours straight doing the princess' bidding was no excuse for her clumsiness. Nor was the fact that she had received in all that time only a few bites of food, table scraps, which she'd taken like a bitch off the floor, cringing on all fours at the dainty feet of her owner.

'Nor can I,' the princess declared. 'You may kiss my

royal slipper while I consider the matter.'

Veeta's lips pressed softly against the woven lavender fibers of the princess' shoe, the same color as her hand-woven dress. Allura could not remember a time when she did not enjoy such scenes; watching slaves and servants alike being humiliated and broken for the enjoyment of one and all.

As the only child of the king, Allura grew up a monstrously spoiled creature, not to mention a pure sadist at heart. She loved nothing more than to see her victims sweat and crawl and beg. As young as five she learned to manipulate events so as to cause these poor unfortunates to be put under torture. It didn't take much to achieve her dark ends. A teacup surreptitiously pushed over the edge of the table, a tiny stone thrown to the ground to be caught up in the shoe of one of the carriage horses, even a bit of mud streaked across her own face or over the lacy hem of one of her dresses were all excellent causes for a beating to be administered to one or more of her attendants.

And if the servants had no chance around her, the slaves had still less. One wrong word from their mistress and they could be sent to the dungeon, sold or even killed outright. If they knew what was good for them they would put much energy into kissing the girl's feet and licking clean her shoes.

For her eighth birthday her father gave her her very own riding crop, a device she used to great relish. It was said that the occasion of that gift marked a day of mourning on the part of the household staff, though Allura herself saw it as the beginning of her true lordship.

The princess also enjoyed torturing the boys her own age, the sons of the nobility. While Allura could not enjoy the thrill of punishing them, she could still make their lives miserable; for defeating her, either in games of skill or chance, was forbidden, as was opposing her physical tyranny. It was quite a comical sight to see the smaller female pushing round the larger males, making them wear girls' clothes and play whatever games she desired.

Had her father seen firsthand the true depths of Allura's cruelties he might well have checked it at a younger age. As it was he was frequently away at war, leaving her care to a great uncle, the Grand Duke Fortragian. The duke took little care in her upbringing, concerning himself with more pressing matters, such as the scourging of lovely peasant women with various rods and canes.

This, too, did not escape the notice of the young princess, who took every opportunity to watch them being brought in late at night. She never saw more than the looks on their faces, their nervous whimpers behind their gags as the soldiers conveyed them on pretty bare feet over the castle floor, but it was enough to make the girl's heart race. Whatever happened behind the closed doors of her uncle's bedchambers, it was serious, important, and above all nasty. Something different from the mere disciplinary beatings imposed on the cringing backs and crimsoned buttocks of the household staff, she was sure of it – but what?

Many years would she have to wait to learn more, and many events would she have to live out. Not the least of which was the sudden and untimely death of her father in a cavalry battle near the southern frontier.

Allura was eighteen when they brought her the fateful news. Her expression betrayed nothing, nor did her mannerisms. They would see no signs of weakness in her, of that she was determined. They would only know a crueler Allura, one more recklessly determined than ever to impose her will upon the world. It had been thirteen months since that dark day and she had yet to break her vow to herself.

'Kneel up slave girl, it is time for us to decide your punishment.'

Veeta obeyed, assuming the required position, back on her heels, her knees wide apart. The slave had no undergarments beneath her short dress, a predicament that left her nether region exposed. She was kept hairless below, another condition of her subjugation. Allura liked that the girl could not conceal her privates. As an owned girl it was right and fitting that she should be on display to one and all. To the men, in particular.

'Hands behind your back,' said Allura, making Veeta cross her wrists as if they were bound. A long time ago, when she and Veeta were little girls, they had been friends. She had been Saraveeta then, daughter of one of her father's nobles. They'd been thick as thieves growing up, till one day Saraveeta took a fancy to a boy Allura liked too. Allura told her father she'd seen Saraveeta kissing the young man, which was a lie, but a very important lie because by the laws of her people a woman could only kiss the one male who was to be her husband.

The young man had refused the union, which left Saraveeta in the unenviable position of being branded a harlot. The only two possible sentences were death or imbondment, but at Allura's entreaty the girl's life was spared, and now Saraveeta was her old friend's slave.

'What do you think should be done with you, slave girl?' Allura asked, having fetched the sleek black crop of the type used by the jockeys in the royal races.

'Whatever mistress desires.' Veeta's eyes were moist. Her suffering, as always, was great. Hungry and tired and afraid, she must now take responsibility for her own unjust sentencing, punishment for a crime she could not have avoided.

'How cooperative you are all of a sudden,' Allura scathed. 'Now that I am holding the whip.'

Veeta did not flinch, even as Allura flicked the tip of it over her thinly covered nipples. 'Yes, mistress.'

Allura struck her bare arm, leaving a welt. 'Remove your garment.'

Veeta pulled the rag over her head without hesitation. She was a disciplined girl now – an obedient girl.

'What are you, Veeta?'

'A slave animal, mistress.'

'Hands behind your back, slave animal, where they belong.'

Veeta snapped them back into place.

Allura regarded her, making her feel like the subhuman creature she was. 'You are dirty, Veeta. Your hair needs washing. One can scarcely tell where the dirt leaves off and where you begin.'

'Yes, mistress,' said the once proud, raven-haired girl.

'Do you think you are attractive to males, Veeta?'

'I do not know, mistress.'

It was an honest answer, but Allura struck her savagely across her breasts anyway. 'You are suitable only for sex, Veeta. For rutting like a pig. Like a little bitch whore. Do you think that makes you attractive?'

'No, mistress,' she whimpered from the pain.

'Would Porfino want you now?' She named the boy they'd once fought over. 'Except as a convenient cunt?'

'No, mistress.'

'That's what you are, Veeta. A cunt. Say it.'

'I am a cunt, mistress.'

'Very well, let us settle on your punishment. Which do you think is better suited to a lazy slave cunt who can't even count to ten thousand – a sound beating or a good old-fashioned mass fuck?'

Veeta's face grew pale. 'I... I do not know, mistress.'

Allura laughed with cold disdain. 'Of course you know, slave bitch. You're just afraid to say it. You try to fool me into thinking both possibilities disgust you, when in fact you want it all – an ass-whipping and a mass fuck. Go on. Admit it. In fact, I could have you shipped to the frontier and given to the barbarians and even that would arouse you. I hear they know how to treat a woman – an enemy woman.'

The girl shook her head. Allura's threat was a new one, saved for a special occasion. Veeta seemed like she might break down, something that hadn't happened in some time now. 'P-please,' she said, her voice shaking, 'don't do this... if our friendship means anything to you, Allura.'

Allura's features darkened. The little slut had pushed it too far this time. 'On your back. Fingers in your cunt.'

The girl gave a little moan but moved to obey, spreading her legs wide so as to allow herself maximum access. Nothing made Veeta more vulnerable, and therefore more enslaved, than forced self-pleasuring.

'Pinch your nipple, touch your clit.'

Veeta writhed at her own touch. How disgusting, and yet how totally provocative. In a way Allura envied her the freedom she had, to be naked like that, with no responsibility, no accountability and no reason to hold back.

'Now tell me, Veeta, how does it feel when you're being beaten?'

'I get all hot and wet, mistress. Even when it hurts very much... especially then.'

'You like the whip on your skin, don't you?'

'Oh yes, mistress,' she sighed. 'It burns me and brands me, it makes me feel... like a woman.'

'And the cane?'

Her eyes glazed over. 'The cane is so hard and brutal, mistress. There is nowhere to hide when it comes smacking down on my behind. I have to take it. I have to absorb the blows, and afterward, the marks. I run my hands over them sometimes when no one's looking.'

'But you like getting fucked, too, don't you?'

Veeta arched her back, pressing her pelvic bone tight to her fingers. 'Yes,' she hissed. 'Oh, yes.'

'Tell me,' Allura demanded, seeking enlightenment for her virgin ears. 'What is it like to be with a man?'

'Men are strong, mistress, they take what they want.'

'And you must give it, for you are a slave.'

'Yes,' she tremored, on the brink of orgasm.

'You may not come,' said Allura cruelly, 'or I shall have you sent to the barbarians, to be their sex toy. On the other hand, if you stop touching yourself I will have you impaled.'

Veeta whimpered, knowing the impossibility of her predicament. 'Mercy, mistress, please.'

'No,' said the petulant princess. 'Not till we've finished our discussion. Do you like being a slave girl?'

'I have no choice, mistress.'

Allura bent down, whip in hand to lash at the girl's thigh. 'That is no answer.'

'S-sometimes,' she tried again. 'I like to be a slave sometimes.'

'Legs wider apart, bitch, and pinch those nipples.'

Veeta struggled to perform as ordered. The conversation, the game, was hardly new. They enacted it often, for Allura's enjoyment.

'We were rivals once. You liked to tease the boys with your body.'

'Yes, mistress.'

'You teased Porfino, for example.'

'I did, mistress.'

'You are no longer a tease, are you, Veeta?'

'No, mistress.'

'At the snap of my fingers you would crawl to any man's belly and beg him to use you.'

'Yes, mistress.'

Allura chortled with satisfaction. 'Tonight I shall have you fucked by the guards again. You may thank me in advance.'

'I-I thank you,' she shuddered. 'For having me fucked, mistress.'

'You will enjoy it.'

'Yes... my mistress.' Veeta gasped. The convulsions were upon her. She would not be able to hold out much longer. 'Please, mistress, I beg to be allowed to come.'

'You will have plenty of chances to do that with the guards, won't you, you lazy bitch?'

Veeta's whimpers grew piteous. She shivered, writhing uncontrollably, her own fingers like fearsome invaders to her sex and breasts.

'You are making a mess on my floor.' Allura noted the glistening juices leaking from the girl's crotch onto the marble. 'When we are done you will lick it clean with your tongue.'

'Yes, mistress.'

Allura felt the heat between her own thighs. There was a fevered light in the slave's eyes. Something wicked she'd seen many times before. It occurred in her suffering, in her sexual distress. How could this be possible, that the two, pleasure and pain, could be linked?

'Get up,' the princess commanded, lashing the girl furiously. 'To the columns with you. Show me what a little whore you are.'

Veeta did not need to have the order spelled out. She

knew well what it meant to be ordered to the row of fluted marble columns ringing the princess' sunken bathtub. She pressed her body against the first one, grinding as though it was a man. Few punishments were more humiliating to Veeta, or more pleasurable to Allura than this one.

If denying the slave orgasms was one form of torture, so was compelling them. And yet the desperate girl was more than willing to trade her pride for a chance to rub her breasts, belly and cunt against the cool, rounded surface. The first climax was upon her almost as soon as she clutched the column between her thighs. Wrapping her arms tight, she pushed her nipples savagely against it, allowing maximum friction.

In the beginning Veeta had cried and begged not to be forced to do this, especially when ordered to do so in full view of members of the household staff or guests. The whip, however, proved a very persuasive teacher, as did hunger and other tortures, too many to mention. But being a smart girl Veeta learned quickly that humping a column like a dog was by no means the worst thing that could be done to her enslaved flesh.

Sometimes Allura liked to make her hug the column while being whipped. This way Veeta would experience sweet stimulation and agonizing pain. Perhaps now would be such a time. She need only decide on the correct instrument of punishment – one of the snaking whips, perhaps, or the dreaded cane…

The princess' reverie was interrupted by a knock upon the doors of her outer chambers. 'Who is it?' she raged, determined that someone should pay for this interruption. 'Who dares disturb me?'

'Forgive me, princess,' came a voice she knew at once to be that of Meksior, the spineless vizier to her Uncle

Fortragian. 'I have come to inform you that your visitor has arrived.'

'Visitor? What are you talking about? I am expecting no visitors.'

Veeta continued her heavy breathing as she pushed herself to another humiliating orgasm.

'Count Raysar, princess. The latest suitor. You recall his appointment?'

The suitor. Yes. One of her uncle's ideas. The grand duke, now regent of the realm, intended to marry Allura off so as to free himself of the problem of royal succession. By law she could not assume the crown herself unless married. It was a ridiculous practice and she intended to alter it at the next convocation of nobles. The princess would marry no one. She would be queen alone. In the mean time, she was humoring the grand duke, interviewing various prospective husbands, each of whom she promptly ran off, tail between his legs.

None were worthy of her, and she was systematically proving her case. This Raysar, whoever he was, would be no exception. In fact, she would see to it his humiliation exceeded that of all the others combined.

'Very well, Meksior, I shall deign to see him. Send him in to me at once.'

There was a judicious pause, followed by the clearing of the vizier's throat. 'Princess, I am not sure it would be proper for the prince to meet you here… in your private chambers.'

Allura stormed to the doors and flung them open. 'Fetch him this instant, you imbecile,' she commanded to his cringing face. 'Or I shall have you drawn and quartered.'

'At once, princess.' He cowered behind his purple robes, nearly tripping over himself in his effort to make it back to the stairs. A few moments later he returned with a high-strung young man, about six foot tall, thin and blonde with nice enough features and white teeth. The fact that he was uncomfortable meeting his potential bride in her bedroom was more than a little obvious, and she could hardly wait till he saw Veeta in the next room.

'Leave us,' the princess said to the vizier, denying him the chance to conduct a proper introduction. Then without further ado she closed the chamber doors, sealing them both inside. Let the games begin, she thought.

'Princess,' the count bowed awkwardly, 'if you will allow me the honor of introducing myself, I am—'

'I know who you are,' she snapped. 'And we both know why you're here. I'm to evaluate you as a potential husband. In order to do this, I'll need to consider many things. Not least of which, I'll need to know how you fuck.'

His features whitened to the shade of a ghost. 'B-begging your pardon, princess?'

'Veeta,' she called out, 'get out here on the double,' and the girl scurried into the room, falling to her knees before her mistress, then without being told she lowered her head to the marble floor and began to kiss her mistress' slipper.

'This is my slave girl,' Allura explained, 'and I would like you to fuck her while I watch.'

Raysar's mouth hung open in shock.

'Well you can't expect me to lay for you myself. I'm a virgin. So you'll fuck her in place of me and that will give me some sense of your skills. Bearing in mind, of course, that this is an owned bitch whom you may treat with as much brutality as you like whereas I am a princess, whom you will have to worship on bended knee.'

Raysar swallowed hard, sweat beading his forehead. 'I believe this to have been a mistake, princess. I regret any inconvenience,' he bowed, his retreating back colliding with the door.

'Count, surely you are not afraid of a mere slave?' A simple snap of her finger was all it took to set the highly trained girl in motion. Without hesitation Veeta lowered herself to her belly and began to crawl to him. Count Raysar, mesmerized by the sight of her undulating, captive flesh, marked as it was with the whip, decided to wait and see what would happen.

'Master,' said the slave, her face at his feet, 'the slave Veeta begs to give pleasure.'

Raysar stiffened as she began to kiss and lick his boot, and Allura suppressed a smile as she watched the swell in his breeches, indicating that indeed he was enjoying the servile behavior.

'On your knees, Veeta,' she ordered. 'Show our guest what you are good for.'

Veeta knelt up, breasts thrust out, back straight. She was a sex slave, which meant there was no mistaking what she must do. This, too, was an act the noble's daughter had balked at when first she was made Allura's bondservant. Never would the princess forget the look on the sweet girl's face when she was first pushed to her knees in front of their mutual friends, pressed by the princess into service for the occasion.

'I would rather die!' pretty Saraveeta had screamed.

'We shall do you one better,' Allura pronounced, sentencing her to a week in the dungeon, a place which makes even the strongest soul beg for death. Chained and naked, the girl was left to lie upon the cold stones in the darkness. Shivering and terrified she could only watch as beady red eyes peered at her, the sharp-toothed rodents waiting for a moment of weakness on her part. There were men in the dark dungeon, too, hungry for bread, and even hungrier for the tight channel between a girl's legs.

For a while Veeta managed to keep herself safe in a corner, out of the range of the shackled prisoners and the rats alike. But then, out of sheer exhaustion, she'd fallen asleep, only to awake feeling something nuzzling between her legs. It was one of the rats, pushing its snout deep inside her sex.

Veeta scurried to the men, begging protection, and knowing that they had her over a barrel, they made her serve them, compelling her to lick clean their filthy feet and cocks before being allowed to lie with them. For the rest of her sentence she was plowed fore and aft, without respite.

Upon being released Veeta showed she had learned her lesson by immediately begging to suck the cock of the young man she'd spurned earlier, but Allura denied her this privilege, compelling her instead to suck the cocks of the stable hands.

'Princess, I must protest,' Raysar objected, though he seemed in no particular hurry either to continue his exit or to hinder the naked girl from exposing his penis and sucking it between her lips.

'Feel free to ejaculate in her mouth,' Allura offered graciously. 'Veeta swallows whatever's she's told.'

'I… I really can't abide this,' the count stuttered, even as he grasped the girl's face between his hands to increase the friction. 'By the gods… this isn't right.'

'Don't tell me you're going to shoot off already?' Allura mocked. 'Surely if you were loving me you'd have more staying power?'

He flushed red. 'Get off me,' he said, not too convincingly. 'Stop this at once.'

'Down slave,' ordered Allura, and Veeta stopped sucking, released him from her mouth and sat back on her heels, just like the good little animal she was.

'By the heavens,' he moaned, knees shaking, and just as Allura had hoped it was too late for the young man; he was going to ejaculate.

With both hands gripping his erection the count erupted, the thick stream pelting the tummy, breasts and face of the kneeling slave girl. Veeta made no move to shield herself, nor did she close her eyes as yet more coated her brow.

'This isn't possible,' he gasped, looking down at the straining tip of his expended organ, but Allura was more interested in the sperm that had dripped onto the floor.

'Lick it up, slave,' she commanded, and Veeta bowed to all fours, lapping at the sticky discharge. 'What do you think, slave; would he make a good husband or no?' Veeta continued to lick the floor, the question rhetorical, for she would continue with the task until told explicitly to stop.

'I do not think you are in need of a husband, princess,' complained the affronted Raysar, 'but rather a keeper.'

Allura made no effort to hide her contempt, or her amusement. 'Be gone, little man.' She waved her hand. 'Before I grow angry with you.'

He left in a huff, not bothering to fasten his trousers. Pity the poor servant who had to point that out to him downstairs.

'And that, my dear Veeta,' Allura collapsed on her bed, exhausted from her labors, 'is how you handle a suitor.'

Chapter Two

'But uncle,' whined the princess, having been summoned by her uncle to his study, 'I don't wish to see another suitor today. I am tired.'

The Grand Duke Fortragian fretted visibly behind his thick white mustache and muttonchops, the weight of his responsibilities heavy upon his heart. 'Grand niece,' he pleaded wearily, 'must you fight me in everything? Have you not had your way in all things? Even more so now that your dear father is passed?'

Allura pouted sulkily. 'I haven't gotten my way at all. It's only because of you that I am entertaining these ridiculous suitors in the first place. The least you can do is let me meet them where and when I choose.'

'And with all the others, yes, that was true. But Baron Montreico must be the exception.'

Allura looked upon the graying, wrinkled man before her, a fraction of what he had once been in his handsome blue uniform. How easy it would be to defeat his will, and yet it was true that as the soon-to-be queen she must learn to be gracious to her subjects. 'Very well,' she raised her nose haughtily, 'I shall deign to meet him in the audience hall. He may have ten minutes, no longer.'

'Ten minutes,' he nodded, obviously relieved. 'Thank you.'

'Do not thank me so quickly. I merely said I would meet him. You can rest assured I will scarcely tolerate him, much less allow him to ever take my hand in marriage.'

'Speak to him,' the duke effused. 'That is all I ask.'

Allura narrowed her gaze suspiciously. 'Why is this man so special?' she demanded. 'What are you hiding from me?'

'Nothing. Not a thing. Come.' He ushered her towards the audience hall. 'The baron awaits you.'

She stopped in her tracks. 'What do you mean, *he* awaits *me*? Do you mean to say he is already in the audience chamber?'

This was indeed an outrage. As princess, she should be allowed to take her place first on the dais, so that he might present himself at the throne and bow to her as was her due.

Fortragian laughed a little nervously as he took her arm. 'Really, Allura, it is nothing to be concerned about. As you said yourself, you will speak to one another for only a few minutes.'

'Even a few seconds is too much under such horrid circumstances, uncle, and you know it.'

'The time will fly,' he promised, as a pair of liveried servants pulled open the doors to the chamber with a crisp flourish.

'Until later, then,' he bid her farewell, medals jingling on his gold embroidered jacket as he scurried for the cover of his study.

'Ever the brave one,' she muttered, observing his comical flight from the theatre of battle. She had been prepared for almost anything as she walked into the marble-columned room with vaulted ceilings and ancient hanging tapestries, but what she saw moved her to an unprecedented level of indignation and outrage.

The baron was sitting on the throne. Her father's throne.

'How dare you?' she cried, storming to the dais. 'I shall

have you put to death for this!'

The Baron Montreico, a booted foot resting casually over an arm of the carved marble seat, merely smirked in response. 'The death penalty is not for females to deliver,' he stated. 'Especially not insolent little brats like you.'

The Princess Allura was taken aback, if only for a moment. No one before had ever spoken to her like this, affronting her royal personhood, and to make matters worse the dark-haired devil was breathtakingly handsome, with lustrous curls, a thin mustache and rugged features. Allura had never seen anything remotely like him before. He was dressed like a buccaneer, with calfskin boots up to his knees, bright red hunting breeches and a long coat of blue adorned with brass buttons. Across his broad chest hung a sash and he was armed with a shining silver rapier. No dandy or court primp ever dressed this way. Even his hands stood out; manicured but capable, accustomed to hard work. She couldn't keep her eyes off them, most especially because he was peeling an apple, running a sharp knife round and round the smooth fruit.

'Death is too good for you,' she decided, warily testing her limits with the man. 'I think I shall have you whipped instead.'

The baron continued to peel his apple, seemingly indifferent.

'Did you hear me?' she demanded, her voice more shrill. 'I intend to have you whipped, hard enough to make you beg to be put out of your misery.'

The baron at last regarded her. 'And you think yourself equal to that task?'

Allura scowled. She did not like it one little bit when a man called attention to the inherent differences in the power of the two sexes. 'The castle guards shall attend to it, under *my* orders. As punishment for insulting me and for casting injury upon the monarchy by... by lounging on the throne as though you were in some house of ill repute!'

'And have you ever been to one of these?' He arched an inquiring eyebrow.

'I beg your pardon?'

'A house of ill repute. Have you ever been to one?'

Allura scowled. 'Of course not. How dare you even suggest such a thing? Now will you get off the throne or shall I call for the guards?'

Montreico's eyes darkened. 'Do that and I'll gag you.'

'You wouldn't dare,' she snorted, though in truth she had no idea what a man like this might be capable of.

'Try me.'

'You are not a gentleman,' she said. 'You are unworthy of your title.'

'And I suppose,' he laughed ironically, 'that you are worthy of yours?'

Allura flew at him, her temper pushed beyond all limits of restraint. She'd intended to receive the satisfaction of a hard slap to his face, but what she got was the man's hand clenched like a steel cuff upon her forearm, holding her at bay.

'You're hurting me,' she gasped, hiding her shock at being restrained in such a way.

'As you would have hurt me?'

'I hate you,' hissed the crown princess, summing up her emotions in a single potent, if immature outburst. 'And I hope you rot in the dungeon.'

'Be careful of your words,' warned the baron, 'lest you find yourself one day in a position of accountability.'

'Are you threatening me?' she demanded.

'I am not a man to threaten.'

He released her and she rubbed her arm, though it was her pride that was injured more than her flesh. 'When I am queen,' she fumed, 'I will have you fed to the dogs for laying hands upon me.'

The baron rose to his feet, towering over her. 'And when I am king, my dear princess, you shall beg me to lay more than my hands upon you.'

She stepped back to avoid being thrust aside as though she were a mere serving wench, her heart thudding in her chest as she fought to find the words to put this man back in his place. But all she could do was watch him leave, swaggering, the sword swaying at his side, her small fists clenched, her throat dry.

'One more thing.' He turned back. 'You have a slave by the name of Veeta, do you not?'

Allura tensed. 'What of it?'

'She indicates you show an inordinate curiosity in the life of an owned female, what it is like to perform for men, to be beaten and used, and so on. Is this so?'

'I am interested only in as much as I am a slave owner,' she replied, trying not to sound defensive. 'My motives are purely academic.'

The baron smiled condescendingly. 'Indeed. And are you curious as well – academically speaking – as to what I would do with you here and now, if you were my slave?'

'Absolutely not,' she laughed scornfully, even as she felt a strange heat mounting between her thighs.

'Pity,' he shrugged. 'Good day, then.'

'Wait, baron...'

He was nearly at the door. 'Yes, princess?'

'Tell me,' she blurted impulsively, 'what you would do to me.'

'To begin with, I would strip you naked,' he declared. 'I would then order you across my lap and spank you for your insolence. Sufficiently humbled, you would be set to work. Picking up those apple peelings, perhaps in your mouth, on hands and knees. You would then give me pleasure, swallowing my issue, knowing that afterward you would be caged for the night like a dog, denied food and water till you begged to be allowed to serve me.'

Allura's knees grew weak. 'You are a pig.'

'No,' he grinned, 'I am a man.'

A few moments later he was gone and she was alone, and for a long time she stared at the peelings deposited upon the dais. The room seemed full of the baron's presence still. She could smell his scent. She could see his eyes, so deep and penetrating. And his words, so scandalous and cruel, still echoed in her ears. The things he would do to her. Impossible, horrible things, done only to a slave.

What would it be like? What if he had the power to compel her to remove every stitch of clothing and order her, naked, across his knee, her belly pressing to his red breeches, her ass utterly vulnerable to those masculine hands? Her pulse raced as she gave in to her forbidden thoughts. Desperately, her hands molding her own buttocks, she tried to imagine what it would feel like to be disciplined, to be taught obedience by such a cruel and powerful man. He would be merciless, that much was clear. He would redden her behind, smacking it over and over until she had no option but to beg for mercy.

He would eventually stop, but only when he wanted. Her tears would mean nothing. How would it feel to be treated so harshly, only to be forced at the conclusion to retrieve apple peelings with her teeth?

She had to know. She had to experience it, now, in the safety of her aloneness. Slowly, very carefully, feeling weak and hot, she lowered herself to her knees, and then to all fours. How cold was the marble on her palms! Was this what it was like for Veeta every time she had to crawl?

Slowly, deliberately, Allura inched forward, the nearest apple peeling seeming to mock her, repeating the man's words.

She would pick them up in her mouth, he had said, with the full knowledge that a cage awaited, and with it an endless life of suffering and obeying. She trembled as she lowered her face, using her lips she picked up some peel, and as she bit she wondered why a mere apple had never tasted so rich and alive before?

She was cleaning the floor, she told herself, on her hands and knees, using her mouth like a slave to remove a man's careless waste. Allura pressed her thighs together. She was wet there. A little more friction and she might even come... but it was then the shame of it all over came her, and hastily rising to her feet, spitting out the horrid piece of the baron's garbage, she bolted from the room.

'I want that floor scrubbed,' she cried out to the nearest servant as she ran for the stairs. 'Have Veeta do it. Naked. On her hands and knees. Then send her to me!'

The princess did not breathe again till she had closed herself in her chambers and thrown herself on her bed. What had she done? And more importantly, what did she almost do?

The very next morning the princess had Veeta strung up by her wrists to be whipped; punished for speaking to the baron behind her back.

'When did he approach you?' Allura demanded.

The naked girl hung her head. 'It was only yesterday, mistress. He intercepted me as I was fetching you tea. I am sorry I spoke to him, but he commanded me. What could I do?'

The princess struck at the slave's breast, smooth and completely defenseless. The resulting welt was in good company with the many others she'd already suffered.

'Do not be insolent with me, little bitch.'

'No, mistress. Forgive me, mistress.'

'What did he ask you about me? You will tell me every detail.'

Veeta hesitated. 'He... he mostly asked me about myself, mistress.'

Allura fumed; how dare he show interest in a little slut like her? 'You? What could possibly be interesting about you?'

'M-my dreams, mistress. He wanted to know my dreams. And my childhood, that interested him too.'

Allura laughed in her face, inducing the hapless girl to lower her eyes shamefully. 'He is as stupid as he is rude,' she declared. 'Who but an imbecile would care for the dreams of a slave?'

Still, the matter was curious. Was there some weakness on the baron's part to be exploited here? Could it be the man had a soft spot for the little whore with big brown eyes? If so, Allura now had a means to hurt and humiliate him. 'So what did he do when he'd finished interviewing you? Take you for a romantic stroll in the garden, perhaps? Or did he sing you a love song on bended knee?'

If the slave picked up on her mocking tone, she gave no indication. 'No, mistress, he did neither of those things.'

'What then?'

'He fucked me, mistress.'

'F-fucked you?'

'On all fours. He commanded me to the floor then mounted me, thrusting his hard cock inside me, and he erupted, filling my womb with his hot seed.'

The graphic description and the images it evoked were more than Allura could bear. 'You lying bitch!' She struck at the slave's pussy, delivering a cruel slash of the whip. 'A man that powerful would never waste himself on a piece of collar meat like you.'

'Forgive me,' the slave pleaded, 'but it is so. I was fucked on my hands and knees, spilling his noble issue inside my unworthy cunt.'

'Don't make it worse for yourself by repeating your filthy lies!' Allura growled, though she could not understand why she was making such an issue of it. What did it matter to her what a pig like Baron Montreico did with his penis? Should she be surprised he'd sport with the lowest of slaves, even one as pathetic as Veeta? The man was of no significance to her whatsoever. She would never again give him audience nor would she permit him within a thousand feet of her person. Under pain of death. His.

'Chamberlain!' she shouted, tugging loudly on the summoning bell, and a white-wigged man in long green livery entered, bowing at the waist. 'Tell me, chamberlain, are the stable boys working today?'

'Yes, princess, as always.'

'Good. I want you to fetch me one. Any will do. Bring him directly as you find him; make no effort to clean him up in any way. Is that clear?'

'Perfectly, princess.' The man bowed again, taking three large steps backwards before turning crisply.

'I'm going to do you a favor.' The princess ran the leather thongs of the seven-stranded whip over the slave's breasts and belly. 'Since you were yesterday fucked by a pig, I am going to let you graduate today to a smelly stable boy, and as always you may thank me in advance for my ongoing kindness.'

'Thank you, mistress.' Veeta opened her mouth obediently to suck the proffered whip handle.

'Maybe I should have him finish your whipping. Men are ever so much stronger.'

The gagged slave girl whimpered, the sound barely escaping her sucking mouth. She was protesting, but Allura could see the glistening juices between her legs.

'How dare you pretend to be distressed,' the princess squeezed an available breast, 'when it's obvious you love the idea?' Veeta tried to shake her head, earning a heavy smack to her cheek. 'Don't contradict me, you miserable cunt.'

'Princess, the stable boy has arrived.' It was the chamberlain returned with her special delivery, a gorgeous stable boy with ripping muscles and long dark hair, shirtless and wearing tight leather breeches. For a split second she wondered what Montreico's torso looked like under his shirt, how his muscles would be shaped, the strong biceps and triceps and the rock hard abdomen, but quickly she banished the image.

'Stand upright,' she told the bowing stable boy, looking him up and down. 'He'll do,' she decreed. 'You may go, chamberlain.'

'Princess,' he repeated the backwards bow, a move she'd seen so many times in her life it was now more dull than watching a dog scratch its fleas.

The stable boy looked nervously at the departing senior servant. Ordinarily a low level servant like him would go his entire life without ever setting foot in the castle, much less being in the same room as the crown princess, the very daughter of the dear departed king.

'When I am queen, boy,' she informed him, 'I will own everything in the kingdom, including you.'

He swallowed nervously. 'Yes, princess.'

She laughed. 'I'm only joking. For goodness sake, relax. You're here to have a good time.' He was about to have a very good time, one that would surpass anything he was ever likely to enjoy again in his whole miserable life. She hoped he'd appreciate the extraordinary lengths she was going to for him. When her uncle found out about her bringing this male creature into her bedchambers he was sure to give her a stern lecture.

'What you do reflects not only on you, Allura, but upon the monarchy itself. The very future of our realm depends upon your sensibilities.' Those were his watchwords, or a close enough facsimile. As if the man himself did not have his own lowly liaisons, the pretty peasants girls rounded up to take his beatings and whatever else he could manage at his age.

What a caretaker like Fortragian would never understand, though, was the loneliness and isolation of the kingship itself. Her father had felt it and soon she would, too, but in the meantime she planned on enjoying her freedom. As well as practicing in small doses her soon to be absolute power over the whole kingdom.

'Tell me your name, boy, and your age,' she demanded.

'I am Willemo and I have passed twenty summers, princess.'

'That makes you a year older than me. Splendid. Now tell me, Willemo, is that slave hanging there pleasing in your sight? Does she have, in your estimation, a good body?'

'Very much so, princess.'

'You would fuck her, then?'

Willemo's brow furrowed. He was becoming suspicious. 'Princess, if you wish to make some accusation pray do so now and not later.'

'No accusations, Willemo, merely a gift… in exchange for one small favor.'

'Princess?'

'You must whip the slut before you fuck her.'

'But I have never done such a thing, princess.'

'And you call yourself a man?' she laughed. 'Come, fetch the whip from my hand, boy. Veeta wants a taste of it, don't you, slut?'

'Yes, mistress,' rasped the broken girl. 'I beg to be beaten as the animal I am.'

Allura nodded in satisfaction. 'There you have it, Willemo.'

His lips tightened, but he stepped forward to retrieve the seven-stranded leather whip without objection.

'Not there.' She stopped him as he moved to stand behind her. 'You will whip the slut on her breasts and pussy.'

Veeta's eyes watered. The pain would be exquisite.

'And I should like you naked, Willemo, if you please.'

Knowing himself powerless to resist the command of one so powerful, he pulled off his boots and slid down his breeches, his semi-rigid cock a work of art.

'Stand in front of the slut,' Allura ordered. 'Let her see what will be fucking her soon enough.'

Willemo was a big youth, with hairy balls and a sturdy penis.

'Tell me, Veeta, is the baron this well endowed?' Allura enquired mischievously.

'N-not quite, mistress.'

'Oh? And what of his muscles? Do you think he could beat this Willemo in a fair fight?'

'I do not know,' the hanging slave replied. 'I did not get a close enough look.'

'He possessed you, did he not?'

'Yes, mistress.'

'Then I would say you got very close. Willemo, strike her pussy, as hard as you can.'

Veeta cried out at his first attempt, but Allura was not satisfied.

'You must do it harder, Willemo, or I will have you whipped by the guards in her place.'

Willemo reared back his arm and let loose, leaving a savage red mark across her denuded mound.

'Now her breasts,' the princess directed, and the young man lashed out, beginning to get the hang of the device. 'More,' ordered the princess, her pulse racing. 'Hurt her more.'

How Allura wished she had a man's arms, a man's legs and a penis between her thighs to provide the ultimate punishment. 'Where is your baron now to protect you, dear Saraveeta?' she goaded.

'Mistress, please,' she moaned. 'I am yours, only yours.'

'Lying slut!' She grabbed the whip. 'You enjoyed him. You surrendered to him. How could you not with a man like that? How could you not yield and be his slave after just one touch?'

Allura hated her at that moment, more than she had any other human being on earth. What right had she to be fucked by that awful baron, or to give him pleasure? Veeta was her slave, and hers alone. 'I believe today is the day I shall hurt you worse than all the others combined,' she vowed, thrusting the handle into the slave's sex, ignoring her sobs. 'I will use iron rods, I will draw blood, I swear it!'

'Have I interrupted something?'

Allura's skin crawled. It was him, the dark and dangerous Montreico, right behind her. 'You most certainly have,' she whirled to face him, 'and I shall thank you to leave at once.' She was utterly unprepared for the sight of the rakish baron in his uniform of office; a red tunic, gold emblazoned, with black trousers, black boots and a rapier at his waist.

'I shall be pleased to.' He bowed. 'Only there is the small matter of your girl, here.'

'What about her?'

'I should like the pleasure of her flesh once more this morning.'

Allura stiffened in rage. Was there no end to the man's nerve? How could he possibly presume to barge into her private quarters and demand to use one of her personal serving slaves?

'Sir, I shall ask you once more to leave, or else I shall summon the guards to have you removed. And while you are at it, I pray you do not stop merely at vacating my chambers, but rather the whole of my castle.'

The baron regarded her, amused. 'You know, princess, you really are quite charming when you're worked up. I'll bet your nipples are hard, aren't they?'

Allura's first reaction was to attack him again, but she'd learned her lesson from the last time. 'I have nothing more to say to you.' She brushed by him.

'I hope you're not leaving on my account?' he mused, and she treated him to her most charming but dangerous smile.

'Actually I am on my way to my uncle to arrange for your arrest,' she said. 'Good day, baron.' He hadn't any clever retort, which she took as a good sign, and marching straight to the grand duke's study she unleashed her venom without preamble.

'The man is a menace, uncle,' she gabbled. 'He has insulted me for the last time. I want him thrown into the dungeon.'

Grand Duke Fortragian glanced over his reading spectacles at her. 'Niece, have you not the common courtesy to knock before bursting in?' he demanded irritably.

'This couldn't wait.' she folded her arms determinedly across her bosom, the fact that her nipples really were erect secretly adding to her discomfort and fury. She was in no way attracted to the man. No, if anything it was the attractive servant Willemo arousing her.

'All right,' he sighed, putting down the quill he'd been using to sign promulgations, 'tell me what this fellow has done.'

Allura proceeded to relate the entire sordid story, leaving out the salacious detail of her picking the peel off the floor of the throne room with her lips. The grand duke listened implacably, showing no small measure of patience as she made the same points again and again.

'My dear niece,' he said at last when she had wound herself down to where he could get a word in edgewise, 'your father and I took great efforts in your rearing to keep you shielded from many of the harsher exigencies of life, but I'm afraid the time has come to elucidate you on certain political matters. Though it pains me to say so, I am not going to live forever, nor do I have vast power at my disposal to keep the various unruly nobles in line—'

'And that is why you should lobby to change the law so the throne can be turned over to me, so I can deal with them,' she blurted.

Fortragian held up a hand. 'Interrupting your elders, young lady, is hardly a sign of royal maturity.'

The princess pouted.

'Baron Montreico, coarse as his behavior might be, is a great ally of this throne, Allura. He has armies at his disposal and he is, at the moment, an indispensable part of my plan to insure you have a kingdom left to preside over. As for your ruling alone, we have been over this already. You must have the protection of a husband or the nobles will eat you alive.'

'It is I who will eat them, uncle. This Montreico for starters.'

'Niece, I beg you, simply tolerate the man while he is here. I am not asking you to marry him.'

'Good,' she said. 'I would sooner marry a warthog.'

The grand duke pursed his lips. 'He does not seem so objectionable to me. I see the way the maidens look at him, and the slaves cannot crawl to him fast enough.'

The princess turned her nose up. 'The man does nothing for me, now if you will excuse me I think I should like to attend to my slave.'

'We shall see you at dinner then,' the grand duke reminded. 'At eight promptly, if you please.'

Allura nodded her affirmation and was off again in a bustle of pink skirts. So she must endure the presence of the baron. Fine. That did not mean, however, that she must in any way acknowledge his existence as a human being. Let him try a dose of her cold shoulder treatment and the man would quickly be sorry for his outrageous behavior. By the time she was done with him, in fact, the man would wish he'd gotten off easy with a nice stay in the dungeon.

In the meantime she would continue her interrogation of Veeta, and may the gods help that man if he was still malingering her bedroom when she got back up there.

Which he was, being salaciously pleasured.

'Allura,' he beamed, lounging in one of her gilded wooden armchairs, Veeta between his outstretched legs sucking noisily on his manhood. 'I was hoping you'd return to join us.'

The princess felt the blood drain from her face. Never in her wildest dreams had she imagined such audacity. It was one thing for her to torment men this way, but no one had ever dared take such liberties with her.

Montreico pulled a cigar from his tunic. 'She's quite a good little cocksucker, isn't she?' he mocked. 'Would you have a light, by any chance?'

The princess fought to keep her eyes off the man's glistening cock, sliding in and out of the slave's mouth. The baron had tied her hands behind her back, which made it more challenging for her to keep her balance.

'Baron Montreico,' Allura declared, refusing to yield to her passions, 'if you have any honor at all, I demand that you remove yourself from here at once.'

'Before I've come?'

'Get out, baron, now,' Allura snapped. 'Do you hear me? Veeta, get away from him this instant.'

The baron held the slave in place as she tried to rise. 'Stay where you are, Veeta.'

'She is my slave,' Allura grabbed the girl's dark hair, 'and I forbid her to give you pleasure.' Veeta cried out as the princess pulled her by the hair away from the baron's erection. 'Now get out, damn you!' she ordered the man, the girl trembling at her feet.

'Am I not a guest of this house?' The baron enquired, seemingly unperturbed.

Allura's mouth watered at the sight of the pulsing, abandoned cock. 'According to my uncle,' she said acidly, 'not me.'

'But your uncle is head of this royal house, is he not? Therefore I am a guest by law, entitled to all that this house has to offer, including the pleasure of its slave flesh. Now unless you wish to take this girl's place I suggest you return her to her task forthwith.'

The logic was as flawless as it was galling. 'Very well, you two deserve each other,' Allura hissed, shoving Veeta forward onto her face.

'You have five seconds to return to your work.' The baron ignored her, speaking directly to the bound slave, who contorted herself, repositioning her mouth. Allura had never seen the girl perform like this, with such perfect fear and obedience.

'I hope it falls off, Montreico,' she said sulkily.

'Your kindness overwhelms me, princess. Now, about the light for my cigar?'

Allura fetched a candle, determined to maintain her aplomb. 'Exactly what do you have on my uncle, anyway?'

'Have on him?'

'Yes. Why is he so afraid of you?'

'I don't know. Why are you so afraid of me?'

'Me? Afraid? Hardly,' she scoffed.

'If you would do the honors.' He indicated she should light his cigar with the candle resting on a nearby table.

'Why not?' she smiled, intending to burn him with it, her plan to drip wax on his cock, but too astute he grabbed her upper arm and knocked the candle to the floor, her protests instantly smothered by the kiss, aggressive and punishing, his grip like iron, his lips hot and pliant. Allura let forth a moan, only to have her mouth plundered by his tongue. Her oversensitive nipples flared again, as did the delta between her legs, and by the time he released her she was moist, her thoughts focused entirely on lovemaking.

'B-baron,' she panted, her eyes heavy with desire. Had he any idea what he'd done? There was no denying the meaning behind his action. If he were to denounce her now her life would be effectively over, regardless of her actual culpability. And yet at this moment she didn't care. Not when there was the chance to be kissed that way again.

'My initial assessment was right,' he rejected her coldly. 'You are a frigid bitch.'

Allura's lips trembled, her reverie shattered. Never had she been so humiliated in all her life. Lacking the will to slap him or even call him any names, she turned away and ran as fast as she could.

Trembling like a leaf she shut herself in one of the empty guest chambers, and it wasn't until she'd locked the door that she allowed herself to fall apart, her tears, long repressed, falling like raindrops as she flopped sorrowfully on the bed.

Chapter Three

Allura would have preferred to do almost anything else that evening than attend a state dinner. It didn't matter that her new white gown with woven silver silk shone like the moon, or that her hair sparkled like the sun; everyone already knew she was the most beautiful girl in the kingdom, so why devote another dreadfully tedious evening to confirming it?

Especially when she was so distraught about her latest incident with Montreico. The man had kissed her, and worse, with disdain, as if she were a mere whore. And then to tell her she was frigid, as if she were supposed to melt on the spot and spread her legs for him in exchange for a kiss.

He was the frigid one, not her. She felt nothing from his forbidden touch. Well, almost nothing. All right, so she'd been worked up all afternoon, her pussy alive, strange images filling her head of being under the man's wicked power, of having to do his bidding, sexual and otherwise. Things Veeta was forced to do on a daily basis because she was not free and had no rights over her own body. It was ridiculous, of course, and the sooner the man was gone from the castle the better.

She would count the hours – as would Veeta, who'd be spending her time in the dungeon until his departure. The girl had begged not to be cast back down there, and it was true, there was no good reason why the relatively obedient slave should be, but Allura was determined to cheat the baron of his slut, and she'd provide the same treatment for any of the other female slaves he took a shine to as well.

'Leave me,' she commanded the slave who'd been combing her hair.

'Yes, mistress.' The girl crawled backwards on her knees to the door, and then onto all fours to scamper away. No doubt she was grateful to have avoided any punishment, and Allura didn't even care that she'd missed the opportunity. Suddenly her usual joys of torturing the females in her power seemed to have gone flat.

Looking at herself in the mirror, her hair elaborately fixed beneath the tiara, her ears and throat dripping with perfect diamonds, her luscious bosom subtly accented by the lace bodice of her dress, she could find no flaw. It was almost too easy; every man wanting her and yet so easily disposed of, blown away like dust.

Except for this Baron Montreico. The one man, it seemed, she could not thwart; the one man who held a secret over her; a terrible truth, the reality of a kiss that still branded her lips... and her heart.

A knock at the door interrupted her thoughts.

'Princess, your presence is required by the grand duke,' the chamberlain called from outside the door.

'Tell my uncle I shall come when I'm ready, not before. And do not disturb me again,' she snapped.

'Allura, by the gods, what are you doing in there? I have five ambassadors waiting upon you!'

Her uncle was there too, come to fetch her, so she rushed and opened the door. 'Sorry, uncle, I...'

His frown receded at the sight of her. 'You are fortunate, Allura, to be so resplendent in your beauty. No one will ever fault your perpetual lateness, though it is a character defect.'

'I know, uncle, and I shall mend my ways.' She took his arm, feeling her usual radiant self once more. Let the dullards at dinner be overwhelmed, she told herself. At least they'd provide her with some amusement as she obliterated them. 'I trust you've devised your usual ingenious seating plan, uncle?'

'Funny you should say that, niece.' He stopped at the head of the table, where he himself was to be seated. A hundred men and women bowed in unison, their garb representing a dozen provinces and twice that many foreign countries. 'I should like you at the far end, Allura, beside the baron.'

Montreico strode forward to fetch her. He wore a uniform of black, with a gold sash and buttons. 'I am honored, your excellency.'

How appropriate, she thought, black for a man with an infinitely dark heart.

'It is you,' Fortragian countered, shaking his head amiably, 'who honor us.'

'Princess?' The baron extended an arm, a self-satisfied expression on his face.

'Certainly,' she smiled back, her poison-filled eyes containing her real sentiments, 'I'd be delighted.'

Every head followed their progress down the table; no doubt the fools expecting an announcement of marriage at any moment.

'I don't know how you arranged this,' she whispered from the side of her mouth, 'but I promise you, you won't get away with it.'

The baron held her chair for her, pushing it in behind her. 'Surely you're not as disappointed as all that?' he whispered in reply. 'I'm exactly the challenge you need. The only one who'll give you a run for your money.'

'You flatter yourself, baron. Anyway, I'm a frigid bitch,

remember? Why would you waste your time?'

He sat beside her, unfurling his napkin with a flourish. 'Frigid bitches are my specialty, princess. You are not the only one who enjoys a challenge.'

'The only challenge you pose for me is finding a means of extermination for so large a rat.'

'You pain me deeply. Wine, my dear?' The baron leaned across to fill her glass without letting her accept or decline.

'If you think getting me drunk will allow you to—'

'What fragrance is that?' the baron cut her off, making a show of sniffing the air. 'It seems strikingly familiar.'

Allura clenched her legs in horror. There was no way his olfactory glands could be that sensitive. She'd bathed afterwards, for goodness sake.

'Yes,' he wrinkled his nose, inhaling again. 'I'm sure I'm smelling something quite distinct from the fragrances of our dinner.'

'And I'm sure I don't know what you're talking about,' she said, without conviction. It had only been a brief dalliance – although highly arousing – before her bath.

'Give me your hand.'

'Let go of me.'

'Aha,' his nostrils flared, her fingertips just under his nose. 'As I suspected, you've been masturbating.'

'Quiet,' she hissed fiercely. 'Do you want to mortify me in front of half the nobles in the realm?'

He appeared to consider the matter. 'Perhaps. Unless you're prepared to provide me with some greater thrill later tonight?'

'Montreico, I beg you, do not shame me this way.'

'So now you are begging, are you? Fine, I give you my terms, take them or leave them. I shall not reveal your secret, so long as you agree to meet with me later, at a time and place of my choosing.'

'How can I trust you?' she asked.

He laughed. 'More to the point, how can I trust you?'

Oh, how this man infuriated her. 'You have my word. Now can we be done with this sordid discussion?'

'Cheers...' He smugly raised his glass, and Allura touched her own against it, trying to draw as little attention as possible to their private exchange, greatly relieved to see the first course being brought. The more distractions the less likely he'd be to say or do anything stupid.

'Admiral Plico,' said the baron, slipping a hand unseen over Allura's thigh. 'My congratulations on your latest victory over the Nasians. The fewer of those scum scouring the high seas the better, I say.'

The white-suited admiral across from them turned bright red, looking as though he'd swallowed an apple.

'Montreico,' Allura whispered fiercely, trying to dislodge his hand at the same time, 'the Nasian ambassador is sitting right next to you.'

'What? By the demons, so he is. You mean to say you've made peace already?' The baron pushed his hand down between Allura's thighs. 'Why am I always the last to know?'

Because, thought Allura, clamping her thighs tight, he was a pompous, ignorant oaf without a smidgeon of worldly understanding.

'Princess, were you aware of this development?'

'Yes,' she replied curtly, trying not to squirm. He was attempting to stimulate her through the material of her complicated dress.

'I'm from the backwater,' explained the baron. 'But I do know what I like.' And at the moment that would be her sex, and it was all Allura could do to keep from jumping up. She had no idea it would feel like this – a man's fingers seeking and probing. It was so different than when she did it herself.

'If you resist me in any way,' he leaned over to whisper in her ear, 'I will expose you… fully.'

'But you promised not to shame me,' she breathed.

'And I won't. If you obey.'

Obey. That terrible, charged word; a word for slaves and servants and wives, not for princesses and queens.

'Personally I think it important to open all trade routes,' the baron managed to work his tortures into the larger conversation. 'Don't you agree, princess?'

She managed a weak smile. He was referring not only to economic and political matters, but to her cunt. The pig wanted better access, but better that than having the whole sordid mess revealed.

'Open… yes…' she replied, her heart thumping in her chest. Could they know what was happening; all the nobles and ambassadors and their wives? Did they play games of their own under cover of the tablecloth?

A gasp passed through her, nearly audible as he managed to apply pressure directly to her clitoris. He had her now. One false move, on either of their parts, and she would be coming for him, right in front of every dignitary for miles around.

'Princess,' enquired a particularly nosy duchess, 'is it true that the Lady Saraveeta is now your slave?'

The baron cast a gleeful sideways glance. 'Yes, princess, do tell.'

'It is true.' She drew a steadying breath. 'She was found to be a harlot and I spared her life.'

'Only to send her to the dungeons to rot,' Montreico reminded.

'That is where slaves belong,' she retorted.

He punished her with a flick of his thumb, enough to make her blush and squirm.

'Princess, are you quite all right?' the gray-coated ambassador from Zenuria asked.

'I am quite fine... thank you,' she gasped.

'Perhaps the princess is overcome thinking of the turn of events for her poor friend,' provoked the baron. 'It must be difficult to see the dear girl in bonds, naked, reduced to the level of mere property.'

'Harlots deserve what they get.' The princess was determined to yield not an inch.

'Personally,' said the double-chinned wife of the Zenurian ambassador, 'I find female slavery distasteful in its sexual aspects. It is an encouragement to loose morals.'

'It is true,' said the baron. 'The female slave is a sex toy for her owners. The male may use her in every conceivable manner, and it is not even considered adultery on account of the creature being defined as animal and not human. The princess' friend, Saraveeta – I believe she is simply Veeta now – is such an animal, is she not, princess?'

Allura slightly raised her buttocks from the seat, clenching her pussy muscles, desperately trying to draw in his fingers. If only the fatuous guests were not there and she could spread herself wide, rip off her clothes and let him finish her off. It didn't matter that she hated him; it was sexual and she needed it.

'Veeta is an animal, a pig, yes,' the words poured forth, ill chosen and highly charged, 'and a slut. But she always was easy with the boys. She never was a female, baron, only a slave, from the day she was born.'

Montreico withdrew his hand without notice, and Allura had to choke back the whimper of sudden deprivation.

'And you, princess, are so much the opposite.'

There was a tinge of irony in his voice, enough to give pause to the conversation, and it was resumed again, lightly, only once the soup arrived.

'Do not close your legs,' the baron warned, and the princess sat open, her every nerve-ending alive, every word, every sound and taste connecting directly to her sex. The laughter of the men jarring her, like tremors threatening to knock her from her chair onto the floor at their feet. The clinking of glasses, the aroma of meat from the kitchens drawing attention to her empty belly, her ravenous need to eat, so easily controlled by a single man.

And worst of all, the metal of the soup spoon on her lips making her think of chains. Veeta was chained at that moment, locked in irons in the dungeon below them, her lithe body covered in filth as the bestial male prisoners pass her back and forth; male beasts sporting with a female beast.

For a second Allura felt the gut-wrenching tear of guilt. Were she and Veeta so very different? Wasn't it Allura who'd wanted that kiss from Porfino so badly? Hadn't she practically thrown herself at the boy not once, but again and again? Had she not offered him everything, the full obedience of her body in a vain effort to distract him from Saraveeta, his true love? And knowing herself second best in the end, had she not falsely accused an innocent girl in order to appease her own bruised ego? It was more than Allura could bear.

'Is something wrong, princess?'

She was on her feet, bracing herself at the edge of the table. 'I... I am in need of some air,' she stammered, 'that is all.'

'Baron,' the grand duke called from the far end of the table, 'would you kindly escort the princess to the balcony?'

'I am fine, uncle,' she declined. 'I should like to go alone.'

The baron grasped her elbow. 'I will not be cheated of my end of the bargain, whether or not you leave,' he growled.

'Of course,' she hissed, 'being the son of a demon as you are, I fully expect you to try and collect. Only it seems you have failed to honor your end of the bargain; I have been disgraced, after all.'

'Only if you make a scene now,' he countered. 'Come quietly and all will be well.'

The man was right and for the moment she had no choice but to cede her arm – and a measure of her pride. So consoling herself with all the nasty things she would do to him when she became queen, she allowed him to lead her from the state dining room out to the balcony overlooking the manicured gardens below.

Allura forced from her mind the feelings of comfort at having someone to lean on – a man to take the reins. She could not entertain such a thought now, for it was enough to confront the weakness in her knees, the heat passing from her body to his, so powerful beside her.

'You may leave me,' she dismissed him at the balustrade. 'I am in no mood for company.'

'I shall wait till I am assured that you are well.'

Well enough to run him through with a blade had she the strength of a man, she thought bitterly. 'I think you've foisted yourself on me more than sufficiently for—'

The baron helped himself to another kiss, abruptly silencing her, this second even more intoxicating than the first, his hands at her bare back pressing her close, holding her prisoner. She nearly fainted at the feel of his hardness, the man aroused, as he had been with Veeta, only this time he wanted her. Allura felt her resistance ebbing, and as his hands moved down to grasp her buttocks she could muster no objection, no will to oppose him.

Her eyes closed, and the princess forgot for the moment her loathing of the man, praying it would go on, forever.

'Allura! By the gods and goddesses, what is the meaning of this?'

The princess gasped, panic supplanting her lurid desire. It was the grand duke. 'Uncle, I... I...'

'No,' he silenced her spluttering. 'It is clear enough what has occurred here.'

'The young lady has compromised my integrity,' declared the baron. 'I demand satisfaction.'

'Me?' she shrieked indignantly. 'But it is you who grabbed me and—'

'And what, Allura?' he interrupted. 'Can you prove to your uncle how I forced myself upon you? Or would you rather tell him the truth, how you put yourself upon me, appealing to my natural male desires?'

'Is this true, Allura?' her uncle quizzed, and her pulse raced. She knew well the laws and customs of her people. Without clear and overwhelming proof of abuse the woman was wrong, guilty no matter what the circumstances. Hadn't she condemned Saraveeta in this very manner having no evidence whatsoever?

It was not a fair system, but it was straightforward. So long as the woman kept her distance she had all the power, but once she allowed the breaching of that barrier, though the touch be slight, everything shifted to the male. Her freedom, her very life was in his hands. 'Uncle, you must give me a chance, alone, to explain,' she pleaded, seeking to hide her increasing desperation. 'There is more here than meets the eye.'

'What could there be to explain?' Montreico argued. 'The law is clear. Fortragian, do you not side with me?'

The elderly grand duke frowned heavily. 'The law is the law, Allura,' he decreed. 'I cannot override it, even for you.'

'She is spoiled meat,' the baron pointed out, quite unnecessarily, 'and she has but one chance at redemption; a legitimate union with the offended party.'

Allura's heart seized in her chest. The man couldn't possibly propose marriage, not after all that had taken place between them. 'Uncle,' she desperately babbled, 'I will never wed this man, do you hear me?'

'Allura, the choice is no longer yours. And need I remind you that should the baron refuse you I shall be forced to sentence you to slavery as a harlot?'

'Me, a slave?' she gasped. 'But I am crown princess!'

'If slavery be too good for you there is always the option of death,' reminded the baron. 'And I would be happy to loan my hangman to your uncle for the occasion.'

'I hate you!' she screamed, turning on him with fists flying, but the baron made no effort to stop her pounding his chest, an action that only made her look all the weaker and hysterical.

'I shall have to consider the matter, Fortragian,' he said flatly. 'In the morning I shall give you my decision as to whether I'll have her or not.'

Allura stopped her useless attack, and burying her head in her hands she reverted to the use of tears. In the past it had helped her win her own way, but not now.

'I am afraid I have grown quite fatigued, your excellency,' Montreico said. 'Until tomorrow, then?'

'Very good, baron.' The duke returned his crisp bow, then turning to his niece he said curtly, 'Pull yourself together, girl. You got yourself into this mess. You've no one to blame but yourself.'

He left her alone to contemplate her options. He was right; she must pull herself together. What was she going to do? Drawing a deep breath she gazed into the night.

She could wait until the baron was asleep and slit his throat; she could hardly imagine anyone missing such a man. But what if she should fail in her attempt? Montreico was obviously a cunning and treacherous man, of the sort not likely to be overtaken even in his sleep.

No, if she was to defeat him she must use her wits. She must beat the man at his own game. To begin with, she could be assured he would want her hand in marriage, which must have been his plan all along, to marry into the royal house, to gain leverage over the crown princess. And therein would lay his undoing. The man's greed would fell him. She would make his life a living hell, removing from him every joy until he either begged her to release him from his vows, or to plunge a dagger into his heart to end his misery. In less than a year's time, she predicted, she would be rid of him and sitting on the throne all by herself. Yes, it was the perfect solution. An immediate marriage would make her uncle happy and she would be one step closer to a life free of men all together.

The only small hitch was her confounded libido. She must in no way succumb to her desires. She must never again give in to his kiss or melt at his touch, and she must never, ever, under any circumstances give herself to the brute physically.

It would be a sexless marriage, and if she had to masturbate a hundred times a day or even give her favors over to some male servant like Willemo to keep her lust at bay, she'd do it; anything to keep her freedom, not to mention her chance of revenge.

In the meantime she had in mind a little game – something to ease the worries on her mind. To this end she would need a few of her special devices as well as the helpless body of Veeta the slave.

'We are going to play princess and robber tonight,' Allura told the girl a short while later, in the privacy of her bedchambers. 'Aren't you glad I got you out of the mean old dungeon so we can?'

'Yes, mistress,' said the shivering girl, freshly scrubbed and deloused after her ordeal. 'Thank you, mistress.'

Allura so enjoyed the expressions on the slave's face. Subtle as they had become, and as many times as they'd played the same games, Allura could still count on provoking reactions; a little sparkle in the eyes indicating fear, a slight furrowing of the brow, and of course the inevitable quaver in the voice. This was a fun game for Allura because she got to play a different role. Naturally she was the predatory robber, while Veeta would be the sleeping princess interrupted by the randy intruder. Allura was quite proud of herself for inventing a device to simulate a male member, which she could attach to herself by means of a harness. Made of smooth metal, the shaft was a silver replica of the cock of her father's favorite horse, making it an especially humiliating thing for the highborn Saraveeta, who was in effect being fucked by a horse-cock.

'What does it feel like?' Allura would always ask, and then teasing she would add, 'We should try the real thing, now that we have you stretched so well.'

The silver horse penis was attached to a wide belt, with connecting straps that fitted between the princess' legs, and as an added treat for her she could install various devices that would insure her own continuous arousal while she was fucking the slave girl.

Veeta had been stretched well, indeed, and she could take a substantial amount of the huge cock, in both channels as well as in her mouth.

'You are sucking a horse cock, Veeta,' Allura would

make sure to remind her as she performed on the silver shaft. 'For the millionth time, aren't you sorry for ever thinking you were more lovely and desirable than me?'

Allura readied herself now for their game. In her guise as robber she would sneak into the bedchamber, the cock firmly in place and assault the defenseless princess. For the occasion Allura would dress her childhood friend in a splendidly sheer and regal nightgown, and even do her hair and make-up. This would make Veeta cry, because it reminded her of all she'd lost.

Allura thought it funny to set up these little contrasts. Certainly Veeta was tortured by them, for it was ever so much crueler to wear finery time and again, only to be stripped and forced to eat on all fours from a bowl.

For the night's game she was spending lots of time with Veeta's hair, making the girl sit in her golden chair while she employed the dreaded silver brush.

'The Baron Montreico fancies to marry me,' she told her slave girl, as though it was some free offer she was considering. 'Do you think him a good catch?'

Veeta wore a red negligee, low-cut, barely covering her nipples. The hem rode so far up as she sat that Allura could see her pink lips at the apex of her slightly parted legs. 'I... I don't know about such things.' She looked anxiously at her mistress, knowing a wrong answer could land her an extra beating.

'Is he handsome? Does he make you wet?'

The thighs of the girl clamped together abruptly. 'Please, don't make me answer, mistress.'

'What? Is this modesty coming from a slave?' Allura aimed the brush at her stomach. 'Shall I have your belly sliced open to learn your secrets?'

It was an old expression, symbolizing the brutal nature of slave ownership, but Allura liked it for its literal connotations. If she wished she could disembowel her old friend. For that matter, she could also have her impregnated as a breeder; a fat breeding pig to make more stupid slaves like her.

'No, mistress, forgive me!' She recoiled.

'Talk,' Allura demanded, seizing a silk-covered nipple and twisting it savagely, the slave whimpering and squirming.

'The baron is handsome, yes,' she gasped, 'and he makes me wet, mistress.'

Allura scowled, releasing her. She'd suspected as much. Her worthless slave had a crush. It was no surprise; what other sort of female would want a man of his low caliber? 'How fitting,' she brushed it off. 'You are both pigs, after all.'

Nothing more was said, but Allura continued to ruminate on the matter. Why had she felt a slight tremor in her tummy at the idea of another female liking or wanting Montreico? Why wasn't it fun to play her humiliation games with Veeta, using this particular man as the butt of the joke? 'Get into bed,' she snapped. 'It's time to start the fun.'

Veeta bowed her head. 'Yes, mistress.' The girl knew her part well. Perhaps she even enjoyed some of it. After all, when now did the former Saraveeta get a chance to lie alone and unmolested in a real bed, even for a few minutes? She claimed the huge penis hurt, but Allura thought she was exaggerating. Veeta was spoiled, that was all. Living in the castle was such a soft life for her; she had no idea what other slaves endured.

Allura enjoyed watching her find her place on the bed, crawling so sweetly over the opulent coverings. What a fine little bride she would have been. In many ways she'd even have made a better princess, with her natural grace and ability to charm one and all by her mere presence. Even with Allura's blonde beauty and the servants always creating a fuss about her, there were times when Saraveeta would steal the light from her entirely.

'Toss and turn, Veeta,' directed Allura, trying to make things as realistic as possible. 'You are dreaming of your lover; show me how that looks. He is coming and even in your sleep you are waiting.'

Veeta's eyes closed. She was on her left side, and with the delicate fingers of one hand she drew a line up her naked thigh. Her lips were moist, and she let out a small moan. This was no fabrication, Allura realized. The girl really was imagining a dream lover. Did she think herself still worthy of noble men, handsome dukes and princes to fawn over her? Was she thinking of Montreico, even?

'On your back,' Allura commanded her personal plaything. 'Open your legs and caress your breasts.' The girl obliged, as manipulative as Allura had forced her to become. 'Behold the princess,' whispered Allura, playing the part of unseen narrator beside the bed. 'Imagining sweet bliss. Not knowing the horror approaching.'

The window was open, and a light breeze wafted into the chamber. Allura gazed upon the girl's body bathed in moonlight, transformed into something almost ethereal. 'Touch yourself, Veeta. Play with your clit.' The slave's pussy was glistening, and silvery liquid anointed her fingertips as she touched that magical bud. 'Yes, that's it, think about your handsome prince, he is coming to rescue you, to carry you away on wings of love, his cock inside you as you fly, his lips kissing your breasts, giving you orgasm after orgasm…'

Allura stopped her just shy of fulfillment. 'Enough. Now you are asleep.'

The girl bit her lip. It took all her will power to deny

herself, and laying her hands over her face she pretended to be unconscious.

'Sleep now, my princess.' Allura's voice drifted to nothing, her own sex on fire. She was wearing gloves, boots, and a dagger at her side. She had velvet breeches, the perpetually hard cock strapped into place. Thus would Veeta meet her brigand, again.

First a gloved hand clamped down over the lightly breathing mouth. The slave princess froze and opened her eyes, with genuine disquiet reflected in them.

'Not a word, bitch.' Allura brandished the knife, her body astride Veeta's. 'You'll do what I say and you'll live. Nod if you understand.' Veeta did so. There was nothing fake about the blade, anymore than there was about the reality of Allura's intention to dominate and terrorize. 'Good girl, now lick my knife.'

Allura's insides simmered as the tiny tongue extended to the flat of the blade, dabbing, seeking to appease, seeking to survive.

'You like cock, girlie?' she growled in a deep voice.

'I-I'm a virgin, sir,' said the de facto princess.

'Not for long, eh?'

Veeta grit her teeth as Allura took her breast rudely, twisting the nipple much harder than before.

'That hurts, sir!' the slave wailed, but the point of the knife pressed into the girl's concave tummy, and Allura's heart quickened as she raised the stakes.

'I enjoy hurting disrespectful girls like you. Didn't you guess that yet?'

Veeta shook her head, wide-eyed as a kitten, fresh and innocent. One more thing for Allura to hate: the girl's ability to renew herself through playacting.

Using the knife she cut away the girl's silk negligee. 'Prepare to be fucked.'

'I submit,' Veeta panted.

'Beg to be fucked,' Allura urged, her voice tense with arousal.

'Fuck me, sir,' Veeta sighed. 'Use me as your whore.'

'Too easy,' Allura hissed. 'Resist me.'

The poor slave pushed with her hands at Allura's arms, being careful not to do it too hard, lest she really dislodge and anger her mistress.

'I am too strong for you, girl. All men are too strong. Isn't that right?'

'Yes, mistress… I mean, sir.'

'Open your legs,' the blonde princess ordered, Veeta did so, as wide as she could manage, and Allura pushed the huge phallus home, smooth metal penetrating easily the ripe, ready girl, who took more of it than she ever had before.

'Who are you thinking about?' Allura demanded. 'Why are you so aroused all of a sudden?'

'Please…' Veeta gasped. 'Please, just let me serve you. Use me as you will.'

'You're not getting off that easily, bitch.' Allura pushed down, the adrenalin surging her to an unprecedented level of penetration.

'Mercy,' Veeta gasped.

'Then tell the truth,' Allura coaxed. 'You are so wet because of him, the baron. You are wishing it was his cock invading you.'

'Yes… yes… I crave him, I confess,' Veeta sobbed.

Allura's satisfaction was all too grim. 'Turn over,' she ordered. 'Face down, ass in the air, spread yourself wide.'

The girl did not dare delay a single second, and obediently rolled onto her front. 'I am yours,' she sobbed, no longer sure in what guise to address the princess. 'I submit to you.'

'Liar!' Allura smacked her ass, the force of the blow thrusting the slave forward with a guttural moan. It was a cruel and unexpected strike, but such was the lot of a chattel property, a toy for the enjoyment of the free. 'You pay me lip service. It's that despicable man you want to own you. You want to belong to Montreico.' The princess could not think clearly; was she looking into the soul of the slave or was this about her own secret desires, hidden behind the character Veeta was playing?

'I want to obey, mistress,' Veeta wailed. 'I want to be good. Please, let me be good. Let me be what you want me to be.'

Allura realized at once the futility of her actions. Veeta was indeed the perfect slave now, broken to her will and terrified more of disobedience than of losing her identity. She had no truth of her own, only Allura's. If Allura told her she wanted the baron, than she would. Likewise any other master Allura picked for her.

'There, there,' the princess patted the head of her sobbing pet, 'come and make your mistress happy. Come and suck your horse dick like a good girl.'

Veeta obeyed again, licking, kissing, then took it deep to the back of her throat, and when she looked up at her mistress, Allura paused from her thoughts to praise her. 'What a good little cock sucker,' she encouraged. 'A certain little slut is going to earn a treat at this rate.'

Veeta garbled her thanks as well as her relief. With great passion would she continue to suck and afterward she would beg and sit up panting to take the tiny piece of candy that was the reward for the sexual performance of a slave.

Allura imagined Baron Montreico in the same position; naked and begging to eat from her palm, and the image made her smile. She would conquer the man, just like she'd conquered Veeta, breaking her will and changing her from a proud girl to a cringing slave. Never mind that Montreico was male, twice her strength and hugely more dangerous than Saraveeta. The difference was naught.

Or so she hoped.

Chapter Four

Princess Allura Alesandra de Triante Volucien stood before the royal court in the finest of her blue velvet gowns. She considered it her best color, drawing out most fully her deep, misty eyes. Her hair was arranged to its greatest advantage, in sensual swirls set with diamonds and sapphires. About her waist she wore a chain of silver and a tiny dagger of state, the jeweled one belonging to her grandmother, Queen Aloethia the Pious.

The neckline plunged just enough to reveal her deep cleavage, also drawing attention to the sapphire and diamond necklace, the gems of which had once ransomed an enemy king in the days of her great great grandfather, King Milasos the Wise.

'Do I look presentable?' she'd asked Veeta on her way out of her chamber, the naked slave still exhausted from the night's sexual excesses, and the slave wearily assured her mistress that no woman had ever looked lovelier in the history of the kingdom. Allura accused her of lying to ingratiate herself, and promised her punishment later.

That is, after she'd gotten this charade of a ceremony over with. Montreico had already kept them waiting about in the audience hall, and frankly she found it infuriating she should have to be kept hostage like this. What was the point? Obviously he would offer her marriage and the matter would be concluded.

'Uncle, why do you not send the guards for him?' she asked churlishly. 'Clap him in irons for insulting my person in this way. And yours.'

The Grand Duke Fortragian gave her a cross look, one she'd never seen before. 'That will be enough out of you, young lady.'

Allura bit her lip. The man had told her off, like a common serving wench or a child. If she weren't so shocked she might well be indignant.

'Good morning, grand duke.'

The hair on the back of Allura's neck stood on end. It was him, waltzing into the chamber in one of his absurd hunting outfits, this time a pair of tight buckskin breeches and a loose weave shirt of forest green, the V-neck tied by loose leather strings. He had his sword belt and a medium-sized cutting knife, and clearly he'd been hunting in the early dawn.

'Baron, we are pleased to receive you.' Fortragian offered a low bow.

'We would have been more pleased a half hour ago,' snapped the princess.

'Allura, silence!' snapped her uncle, and the princess, avoiding Montreico's stare as he moved to stand beside her, kept her eyes straight ahead. She swore if she were to see even the slightest trace of his smugness right now she would tear him to shreds with her bare hands.

'Baron,' continued the grand duke, 'if it please you, may I offer you welcome into this hall, the home of the family which has offended you, and may I further offer the deepest apology, as that family's senior member for the dishonor done to you and your house?'

'As the offended party,' Montreico replied, continuing the formal discourse employed in such situations, 'I accept your family's hospitality and apology, as well as the wisdom you bring as senior member.'

'With your permission, then, may we proceed with the

matter at hand?' asked the grand duke.

The baron inclined his head. He smelled of fresh morning dew and of the forest. The scent of manhood, of conquest and of the kill hung about him in a way that made her weak-kneed and distinctly uncomfortable. 'I do grant this permission.'

'Allura, face your accuser.'

She did so, keeping her face a mask. As for Montreico's, why hadn't she remembered it as being quite so handsome, with its etched lines, capable of worry, laughter and, quite likely, deep passion?

'Do you admit your offense, before these witnesses, that you did soil yourself, yielding to your feminine heat?'

The words rankled unbelievably. 'Uncle, you don't expect me to—'

The duke threw up his hand to stop her. 'Enough, niece, my hands are tied. You will do as is required or this matter will be turned over to the magistrate.'

The magistrate; legal redresser for the poor, keeper of the prison court where even an ugly hag could expect abuse not only from her jailors but her defense attorney as well.

'You wouldn't dare,' she challenged, without real conviction, for one look at his aged face said he would. 'Very well,' she huffed, 'I will play your game, but know for the record I think this is all a sham.'

'I am waiting,' prompted the baron, something in his tone making her react.

She took a deep breath. 'I, Princess Allura, of the House of—'

'No title required.' This time it was the baron who interrupted. 'You will use your given name only.'

'Very well,' she said. 'I, Allura, before these witnesses do confess my crime, that I have soiled myself and yielded to… to my…' She balked at the sight of Veeta being led into the chamber on a leash by a man in hunting gear like that of the baron. What was she doing there? 'To my feminine heat,' she concluded.

'What are the details of your crime?' asked her uncle, pretending not to know.

Allura's cheeks flushed; this was exactly where Veeta had stood for her own false conviction, when Allura could barely contain her glee as the girl was found guilty and subsequently rejected by Porfino. Openly sweet young Saraveeta had wept at the reading of her sentence. 'I… I touched this man… Baron Montreico.' She faltered at saying his name, for the shame of arousal being exposed was more than could be borne. 'I pressed my lips, my body against him.'

'Do you, baron, acknowledge this offense?' asked her uncle.

'I do, your excellency.'

'So be it. Accused, state for this assemblage your understanding of the implications of your action, stemming from the unleashing of your female heat.'

Allura's mouth was dry with anxiety. The baron's gaze upon her was so masterful, so utterly implacable. She dared not read into it or seek to understand. 'By touching this man and unleashing my heat, I have disgraced my ancestors and myself. I am deserving of nothing more than slavery and nothing less than death, depending on the d-decision of my judges.' She stammered the last few words, ancient and unchanging, memorized by every child as an early warning against future misdemeanors.

'Accused, by the graciousness of the gods, there is one chance open to you for redemption from your sentence,' her uncle pronounced. 'Should the man you offended claim you as his bride, then you shall be neither killed nor enslaved. Instead, you will be delivered over and made subject to him in all things. Do you understand this reality?'

Allura quavered at the word 'subject'. She had not thought of marriage in such terms. Surely such a thing would be unenforceable. 'I understand, yes.'

'And you further acknowledge that this man is under no obligation to take you? That he may, if he wishes, cast you away?'

Her, cast away? Never. 'I know all this, yes,' she said, somewhat curtly.

'In that case, before the gods and these witnesses,' recited Fortragian, 'I now require you to acknowledge your indebtedness to this man. You must now beseech him.'

Allura drew her shoulders back proudly. Now would she begin to recoup herself; now would she shine as she ought, dazzling the loathsome man and all the others. Surely even the likes of this iron-hearted baron would melt in the face of such a largess on her part. Weak as her position might be, given that the man could have her or not, there could be no mistaking the honor befalling him.

'I, Princess Al… I, Allura,' she corrected herself, 'do beseech you, Baron Montreico, to accept my favors, knowing that I humbly seek to belong to you in the state of matrimony, before the gods and these witnesses, till death do us part.' She paused briefly before adding the following sentiment of her own to the formula. 'Marry me, baron, by the light of my blue eyes under witness of my beating heart, and let us rule together, now and always.'

A murmur went through the assembly, and Allura allowed herself a discreet smile.

'Baron, having heard these proceedings, being aware of your rights and privileges, are you prepared to render your decision?'

'I am,' he replied without emotion.

'In that case,' Fortragian declared, 'I bid you speak.'

'I, Baron Montreico, son of Alexo, do hereby reject this female,' said he, 'in front of any gods and witnesses you may wish to present… now and forever.'

Allura felt as though the floor gave way beneath her, and in a swirl of velvet she collapsed, her attendants rushing to her.

'Good day,' bowed the baron to the grand duke. 'Your hospitality has been most appreciated.'

Allura heard the retreating footsteps. 'Get off me, you imbeciles!' she snapped, slapping away the many hands fawning over her. 'Montreico, I forbid you to leave this room! Do you hear me? I will not permit it.' He had reached the door. 'I… wait, please. Don't go.'

This final entreaty caused him to stop, and he turned, a look of interest on his face. 'What reason have I to stay, princess, when my decision is made?'

'But you must marry me; unmake your decision.'

'Are you giving me an ultimatum?'

Allura's heart pounded. She had not fully realized until this exact moment how little leverage she had anymore. 'No,' she sought to swallow her venom, 'I intend no disrespect. I only ask that we have a chance to discuss the matter. Alone.'

Her head span with ideas. There was much she could offer in the way of bribes. With her at his side, as an ally, he could become king, powerful and effective. And she would rule behind the scenes. But first she must survive as a free woman.

'Anything to be said may be done so in the presence of this court,' he stated uncompromisingly, returning to stand in front of her.

She looked around at the inquisitive, nosey onlookers. A pin could be heard to drop amidst the eavesdropping silence. 'I can give you a kingdom,' she whispered.

'You have nothing to give me, Allura,' he countered. 'You are ruined.'

'I am still the crown princess,' she argued.

'Without my favor you go to the auction block,' he reminded her. 'Or that of the executioner.'

The man was like ice. Would he respond to a show of feminine helplessness? 'Please,' she offered meekly, 'you cannot let that happen to me if you have any honor, any sense of mercy.'

'Mercy?' He laughed dryly. 'Like you showed your good friend Saraveeta?'

Allura reddened in fury. So he knew the story. No doubt the treacherous slave had told him other things besides. 'Just tell me,' she stiffened, 'what I must do. Every man has a price.'

It was a vicious insult and she feared it would spell her doom. But Montreico merely smiled thinly, pirate that he was, and delivered a counterattack, decisive, degrading and absolute. 'We will have a kiss, Allura, and then I shall reconsider.'

'Go to the demons,' she hissed, snatching her head to one side a fraction as he touched her cheek.

'You will look fetching in a collar,' he went on, undeterred.

His touch made her insides melt, but she fought against her traitorous reaction. 'You will die for that insolence, Montreico. Defiling me is the same as defiling the state.'

Montreico retracted the fingers at his leisure. 'I am surprised, Allura, that someone of your intellect should come across now as such a stupid girl. You are not the state. You are a slut; your body is already forfeit, to me or whoever else buys you. The choice is yours.'

Her heart pounded. She ached to swoon into his arms, to be done with the words and simply let him have his way with her, but she was determined to fight him too, and when that was no longer possible, to mislead and deceive. 'One kiss and then we shall marry,' she bartered.

'No bargaining. The kiss is merely the cost of keeping the negotiations open.'

'Very well,' she tried to keep her breathing under control, 'get it over with.'

'No,' he rejected her waiting lips, 'you will kiss me. Passionately and with abandon.'

Her heart caught in her throat. 'But you are asking me to…'

'To appear as a whore before the court?' he supplied. 'But that is what you are. Unless I marry you and make you mine.'

'I hate you,' Allura let him know. 'And I shall always hate you.'

She rose on tiptoes, terrified to encroach the protective distance between them. Far worse than the shame of the act was what it might do to her inside, to that part of her that wanted to beg for him to take her virginity.

He yielded not an inch, forcing her to do all the work, pressing her breasts against his hard chest. The first contact was like the crackle of fire. Instant combustion. She did not wish to yield to passion, but she could not help but crave more.

Montreico seemed so unmoved and unresponsive. She was afraid he did not like it; was she doing it wrong? Did she not know even how to kiss a man properly? But why should she care? If he hated it, all the better. Maybe then he'd just leave her alone and go back to where he came from.

But she could feel his cock now, pressing against her tummy. They were in their own world, just as they had been last night; the court and her uncle gone. There were no disputes, no struggles, only the rightness of physical lust. And she knew that he knew it, too, that she was ready and hot and completely primed. He need only whisper in her ear, or better still just lower her to the floor and she would tear willingly at her clothes, baring herself for him.

But he did not intend to leave her in this world, this comforting place of security under the cloak of his power. He intended to expose her, to humiliate and ultimately conquer her.

'You have my ear,' he whispered. 'Tell me why I should marry you?' He released her panting body.

Allura could barely stand, her breathing labored and her thoughts spinning. 'B-because it makes sense for both of us,' she eventually managed, her voice shaking.

'For you, not for me.'

'But surely you wish to marry the future queen?'

'The woman I marry will please me in bed,' he said. 'That shall be her only purpose.'

Allura swooned. She had no hope. 'Montreico, haven't you made me suffer enough?'

'Actually, I have only begun,' he declared, moving like a wolf to her throat, taking a bite that shivered down her spine.

'Oh, god, no more...'

'Now,' he said, pulling back from her, 'I suggest you attend to your affairs. You have one hour before we leave for my castle.'

'S-so you will marry me?' she gasped eagerly.

'I shall take the matter under consideration. Now go to your room and await my final decision.'

'Send every available servant to my quarters,' Allura told the chamberlain upon entering the castle, having taken a few quiet moments to herself in the gardens, despite the baron having ordered her directly to her room. 'I shall be packing for an immediate departure.'

A confused expression fell across his face. 'But, Baron Montreico...'

'What about the baron?' she demanded, barely able to stand the pronunciation of his name.

'Baron Montreico has already ordered all of your effects to be packed, princess.'

'By what right?' she fumed. 'How dare he touch my possessions?'

'But, princess,' he spluttered, 'the baron said clearly he was your fiancé; surely that gives him the authority?'

A flurry of conflicting emotions lurched in Allura's stomach. So he was intending to marry her after all. She was free – at least from all the others who might want to own her enslaved body. But why had he not told her himself? Had he not just a few moments ago said he hadn't decided what he was going to do with regard to her?

Allura's expression froze in rage as she looked up at the sweeping staircase. The baron's rough and ready guardsmen, forest men in leather boots and breeches were bringing down piles of her clothes. They were carrying them like rags, without the slightest respect for her station or for their exquisite value.

'Put them down!' she cried, attempting unsuccessfully to interdict one after another. 'Those gowns are worth more money than you will see in a lifetime!'

'Do not interfere,' warned the baron, following his men down the stairs as though he owned the place, 'or I shall be extremely annoyed with you.'

'You are a monster,' she spat. 'How can you let them

ruin my finest clothes like this?'

'They'll be fine. Or new ones can be made in their place, if need be.'

She rushed at him, throwing her fists at his chest, but he twisted her easily about, pinning her arm high up her back. 'Let go of me!' she shrieked.

'Not till you stop making a little fool of yourself. Have you no pride?'

'More than you,' she countered. 'Very well, let go and I'll behave like a good little wife. Oh, wait, I wasn't supposed to know that, was I?'

'One day we'll have to do something about that sarcasm,' he said, releasing her.

'You need only cut out your own heart and hand it to me,' she told him, 'and I will be quite calm and pleasant once again.'

It was then that Allura caught sight of the cage being carried down by a pair of burly men. Inside it, wide-eyed and nervous, squatted Veeta. 'What are you doing with her?' she demanded.

'This slave is part of your personal effects,' said the baron. 'I therefore claim her as part of your dowry.'

'You can't have her,' Allura complained. 'I forbid it!'

Montreico laughed. 'You are in no position to forbid me anything, princess. Besides, what difference does it make to you? You can still make use of her services as a handmaiden as often as you like.'

'But you'll have her,' accused Allura. 'You'll *fuck* her.'

'This is what one usually does with slave girls, yes,' he mused.

'Fine, then take her and leave me behind. Since you haven't the decency to accept my offer of marriage to my face, I hereby rescind it. I'd rather kill myself.'

Montreico's eyes darkened, storms brewing behind them

at the mention of death. What nerve had she touched? She dared not think of the real power of this man, the suffering he might have seen or the harshness with which he might be capable of acting. How many had he killed, she wondered, and how many had he seen die at his side in battle?

'You are coming with me, princess,' he said in determined tones that brooked no form of argument whatsoever. 'Either gowned as you are, on your feet as my fiancée, or huddled naked in a cage as my slave. The choice is yours.'

The princess clenched her fists in impotence. He was trying to provoke and she must not give him the benefit of the doubt. 'I am ready to go now; you will take me from here this instant,' she said flatly.

The baron snapped his fingers. 'Rodolfo, take her to my horse. I will be there presently.'

A tall, handsome man in green hunting clothes with a leather belt slung across his shoulder presented himself.

'Princess, are you well?' Rodolfo asked, after Montreico had headed back upstairs, presumably to continue ransacking her belongings.

'I am a bit faint,' she confessed.

'Allow me to help you.'

Allura was grateful for the man's kindness. Taking her by the arm he steadied her as they walked from the castle towards the baron's contingent.

'Is there to be no carriage?' she asked.

'No, you are to ride on his horse.' The man seemed chagrined to offer such poor arrangements, and Allura stored this observation in her head. Perhaps one day she would be able to use his empathy to her advantage. 'I have never ridden so far in such a rough way,' she played upon his apparent concern. 'Especially not... with a man.'

'I have never known the baron to mistreat a lady,' he said cautiously.

'Please, can we stop a moment, I am very weak now.'

'Perhaps I should fetch a doctor.'

She smiled to herself; the man could be very useful. 'No, I'll be fine. I must be strong.'

'I think perhaps you will need a carriage after all.' He lifted her into his arms. 'I will speak to the baron.'

The man's strength surprised her, as did her own response. Cradled, safely enveloped, she wanted him to kiss her, his mustache tickling her lip, his brown eyes darkening with desire. Would he taste different to the baron? Would she melt in his kiss too, or would he yield to her power first?

Allura craned her neck, her eyes closing. She was so close she could feel his breath, and then, at the last possible second he begged off. 'I should get a doctor after all,' he said hastily, setting her down on the grass. 'I'll go at once.'

He put her down and ran back to the castle, and she looked up at the sky, dazed. What had she nearly just done? If she were caught kissing another Montreico would never have her. She'd be ruined, for sure.

The doctor rushed at the head of the pack, the usual gossipers and toadies close behind. The grand duke was there as well, looking very pasty.

'My niece,' he fell to his knees, 'are you all right?' In his eyes was another question: what had he done to her and was it too late to stop it?

'Of course, she is fine,' snapped the baron. 'On your feet, Allura.' She obeyed, and he lifted her by the waist and set her on the white stallion. 'Say goodbye, Allura. The time has come.'

'Uncle,' she cried, denied a final hug.

Montreico swung himself upon his mount, taking his place behind her. 'We will send word of the marriage date, Fortragian. It will be a private ceremony. One representative each from your household and mine.'

The grand duke bowed with the heaviness of a man defeated. He had spared his niece's life, but at what cost? 'Thank you, baron, for your generosity,' he said flatly.

'May our households grow strong together,' Montreico carried on, in a tone that indicated he was expecting a much bigger piece of the pie in the future.

Allura was terrorized by the speed and power of the baron's horse. It was clear to her now that he was a man of moods who did not enjoy being trifled with, especially not by a female. She would have to mark well her limits – where she could push and where she could not.

'You are going too fast,' she complained, and Montreico pulled on the reins, forcing her to grab the horn of the saddle for support as he brought the horse to a snorting stop.

'Continue on, over the next ridge, wait for us there,' said the baron to his men, who were caught just as off guard as Allura, who did not relish the idea of being left alone with him.

'If you touch me I will scream,' she told him, once the others had gone.

Montreico slipped athletically to the ground and took her by the waist, setting her down beside him on the grass. 'Scream as loud as you like,' he told her. 'What a man does with his woman is between him and his gods.'

'You will be cursed,' she promised, 'for taking their name in vain.'

'That is my affair, princess. Yours, for the moment, is the removing of your undergarments.'

'Excuse me?'

'I believe you heard me quite clearly. I want access to your naked sex under your dress, and I want it now.'

Allura took a step back, her head reeling. 'You're a madman.'

'If you seek to escape,' he said quite calmly, 'I will run you down, strip you naked and tie you by the neck to the back of my horse. Is that how you'd like to enter my castle, princess?'

Allura narrowed her eyes venomously. 'You are no kind of man,' she informed him, 'if this is the only way you have to see a woman unclothed.'

The baron winked at her. 'It is not the only way, my sweet, it just happens to be my favorite.' She stared at him in fury. 'And you will maintain eye contact,' he instructed.

Her cheeks reddened; she was losing her modesty in a far deeper way than mere clothes. Reaching under her skirts she tugged at her petticoat and silk underlinings, and pulled them down until there was nothing to cover her. It was a strange, disturbing sensation, to have her gown material against her buttocks and pubis, especially knowing that he intended to bare them to his own infernal ends, whatever they might be.

'Walk,' he said, pointing when she was done.

Allura looked at the meadow beyond the road. There was a single tree in the middle of it. 'What are you going to do?' she asked anxiously.

'Whatever I will,' replied the baron, dispatching her with a swift smack to her shapely derriere.

'Ouch,' she shrieked, 'that hurt!'

Montreico laughed easily, sounding in genuine good humor. 'How you carry on, girl. That was nothing, barely a tap.'

'There won't be another,' she vowed, trudging through the grass and meadow flowers.

'Save your breath.' He took her arm, steering her where he wanted, directly beneath the shade of the tree's branches. 'Now hold up your skirts, facing away from me.'

'I will do no such thing,' she refused, but he shocked her by slapping her face. She was stunned by the sudden assault, holding her smarting cheek.

'When I give an order I expect it to be obeyed,' he said, by way of explanation for his violent action.

Sulkily, knowing there was little choice, Allura turned away from him and lifted her dress, precisely as he'd commanded. She was hardly done fighting him, but it seemed prudent not to press her point just now.

'You have an attractive ass,' he commented, rubbing his hands over it as if warming them. 'A whore's ass.'

'May the Virgin Goddess come in the form of a bird,' she said with deadly ease, 'and peck out your organs one by one over a thousand years of suffering.'

The baron straightened a single finger and pressed, probing the muscle of her anus, then with a gasp she yielded to the disgusting deed and the digit skewered her rear passage. 'You've no idea,' he said over her squeal of protest, 'what you are dealing with. I intend to break you, Allura, but I shall do so with such subtlety that up to the last possible moment you will delude yourself that you're winning.'

'And I will win,' she grimaced. 'Except in your dreams.'

Montreico worked a second finger into her pussy, which was surprisingly and shamefully wet. 'The time has come for your first beating, princess,' he announced.

'Never,' she defied, though at the very mention of physical discipline her sex began to moisten even more.

'Your body craves it, and so does your soul. That is why you behave like such a brat. You have longed for a man to interpret your signals and put you under his yoke of bondage.'

'I crave nothing,' she argued, 'save your slow and miserable death.'

Montreico massaged her clitoris, making her moan against her will. 'I want you to beg for it,' he growled. 'I want you to beg me to stripe your pretty virgin ass until you scream in agony.'

'This is sheer brutality,' she insisted, though she was beginning to writhe with all the energy of a cheap whore.

'I am waiting.'

He removed his finger from her clit, leaving her hanging. She tried to push back against him, but he held her fast until, in pure feminine frustration, she whimpered, 'Please, discipline me... punish me... beat me... I'm yours.'

'Later,' he predicted, smoothing the luscious globes of her buttocks, 'you will deny this ever happened. Your own mind will play tricks on you in an effort to hold on to your sham freedom and I will allow you this, because it pleases me; it is a game I enjoy.'

'I don't understand,' she breathed.

'No, you don't,' he agreed. 'It's not your place to. But I am going to leave you now, and I want you to bend and grasp your ankles. Do not move from that position until I return. I don't care how long that might be. I don't even care if the entire fellowship of the Monastery of St Torondo walk by and call for you to cover yourself, you will ignore them. For that matter, you will ignore even the apparition of one of the gods. Is that clear?'

'Yes,' said Allura, fearing that soon enough she would be calling him sir.

He eventually returned with a switch, fashioned from some other tree nearby. She had no idea how long he'd been gone, only that every instant was an agony, listening for every sound, the whispers of the breeze and – the gods forbid – the sound of footsteps or horses coming along the road.

'Miss me?' asked the baron.

'I might have been accosted,' she complained weakly.

'And that would have broken your heart,' he sneered.

'What are you doing to me?' she asked. 'I've never been—'

The stick thwacked across her buttocks. 'Never been what?'

Allura cried out in shock and pain, and releasing her hold on her gown she fell forward, her hands bracing against the inevitable fall to the ground.

'Get up,' said the baron mercilessly. 'Or you'll endure twice the number already allotted.'

'Y-you mean you intend to do that again?' she queried miserably, looking up at him from beneath disheveled hair.

'Every day for the rest of your life.' He looked down at her grimly. 'Depending on how well you behave yourself.'

'But I'm not a child,' she protested, much of the defiance already gone from her voice.

'That's true,' he yanked her to her feet, pushing her forward against the tree, 'a child would have some inherent sense of right and wrong and would at least try and appease its elders.' This time he would strike her standing upright. 'Brace yourself,' he ordered as he lifted her skirt himself.

Allura placed her palms on the tree and leant against it, feeling the roughness of the bark through the material against her nipples. 'Please don't beat me anymore,' she begged, though it was obvious he intended to do precisely that.

'You will count the blows up to ten,' he ordered, ignoring her pitiful plea. 'If you miss any we will start again from the beginning.'

'You're a monster,' she whispered, as the switch whistled through the air, biting and irresistible.

'You missed the count,' he stated. 'We remain at zero.'

'One!' she cried as the switch bit again.

'You mark well,' he praised. 'Were you a slave I would display you naked in the courtyard of my castle for twenty-four hours after every beating so everyone could enjoy the view.'

'Two,' she gasped, having no time for small talk.

'Whipping a female takes more skill than one might imagine,' he mused. 'I prefer a lattice design myself. Up, down and across, maximizing the placement of the welts.'

'Th-three,' she stammered, scarcely believing they were not yet a third of the way through.

'You are fortunate you are only my fiancée and not my slave. I would not be so lenient with a bonded female.'

Allura shivered. What exactly would he do to a slave under such circumstances? 'I've done nothing to you,' she defied, her breath torn and ragged, 'but you do me a great injustice.'

The baron slashed again, high on her left buttock, too quick for her to respond. 'The count returns to zero,' he informed, enforcing his draconian rules.

'No!' she shrieked. 'I'll never bear it.'

'I'm quite sure you'll manage, my dear.'

As the blows passed one blended into another. Allura heard herself counting afresh, as if she were a third person, observing nearby or floating above. The pain, acute and pulsing, blended with her heartbeat and with her secret lusts. She was intensely aroused despite – or because of – what he was doing to her defenseless body.

'Done,' he proclaimed at last.

'I... I feel strange,' she mumbled, her voice a gasping whisper. Her bottom was continuing to clench, though he'd stopped striking her. 'Baron, what is happening to me?'

'It is the heat of a female in submission,' he casually observed. 'Must I teach you everything?'

Allura felt shamed by her own naivety, and by her reaction as well. If only this man were not such a monster she might be able to express to him her profound need to be held, to be neither judged nor pressured but simply allowed to absorb this most incredible experience.

'We must be on our way to the castle,' he said dismissively.

'I don't think I can walk,' she told him.

'You will walk,' he stated uncompromisingly, 'or I will whip you along the way for incentive.'

Allura gathered herself, facing the depth of her loneliness. Revenge alone sustained her, and the hope of seeing him in her place. If he thought he was heartless, she would be twice as bad.

'The ride will not be pleasant,' he warned as she stood meekly beside the horse. 'Because of your welts,' he clarified.

'I should be allowed in the wagon,' she said. 'My own slave has better accommodations, as do my clothes.'

'Your slave can be thrown to wild dogs at my slightest whim, as can your clothes,' he laughed. 'Is that the status you would like to share?'

'I want my undergarments back,' she demanded, ignoring his sarcasm.

'No, you will ride as you are, and you will not sit on your skirt, either.'

The baron compelled her to sit bare-assed on the saddle,

her agonized buttocks burning from the touch of the leather. 'Hold on tight,' he ordered, his arm clamping her waist and drawing her close. The horse gave a whinny and began to trot, and then to gallop, the moving saddle causing her pain and pleasure in equal measure. The man behind her was overwhelming too, with his scent and his iron will, palpable and deeply sexual. His cock was hard against her lower back, and she had the overwhelming desire to be on her knees, appeasing him with her mouth, her helplessness reinforcing her arousal.

Montreico returned them to the head of his troops. They passed the wagon and she saw the cage in the back was open. She wondered if Veeta was gone, but then behind it she saw the girl's slender legs in the air, a faceless man rutting between them, his naked, hairy ass rising and falling rhythmically, one of the guards fucking her as the caravan moved slowly along.

Rodolfo pulled alongside his commander. 'Baron, do you wish to stop at nightfall?'

'No, we press on. You will ride ahead, Rodolfo. Alert the castle to be at the ready for us.'

Chapter Five

The silvery moon, barely a tenth full, was high above the baron's castle when they arrived. Allura was grateful for the relative darkness to cover her unseemly entrance into the midst of his household. These were, after all, the servants over whom she would soon hold sway as their mistress. Seeing her arrival on the man's horse as disheveled and flushed as she was would have been an uncompromising blow to her authority. She wondered if this was part of the baron's reasoning for riding them so hard in one day.

'Well done,' he murmured to the steed, feeding it a carrot as soon as they dismounted. Allura was starving, but she wasn't about to beg him for food.

'Seeing as how you care so much more for your horse than you do for me, I should like to be shown to my chambers,' she said icily. 'If it's not too much trouble.'

He continued to pat the muscled neck of the horse as he addressed her. 'You will have no chambers, only temporary guest quarters until we are married.'

For the moment Allura had not will with which to argue. 'I am concerned only with tonight, baron. I am very tired.'

'Rodolfo will show you the way,' he said.

'I will require my belongings as well,' she said haughtily. 'And my slave.'

'Your slave is occupied at the moment. I shall have her sent presently.'

Allura bristled. 'Occupied, you say? Don't you mean

she's being abused by your men?'

'She seems to be enjoying it well enough,' he shrugged. 'At any rate, my hands were tied. A few of them made use of her on the way here and now they all want her, so naturally, in the interests of fairness, I have allowed it.'

'Allowed it? But you have no right. She is mine; a lady's slave, meant for a lady's service.'

The baron arched an eyebrow. 'Veeta has told me differently,' he countered. 'She indicated you frequently punish her by throwing her to packs of men. Guardsmen, prisoners, even. And that afterwards you thirst to know every intimate detail of the experience.'

Allura was crimson. Once again he was hinting at her fascination with female slavery. 'I am as far above a slave, baron, as I am above you,' she spat.

'Rodolfo,' he said, infuriatingly ignoring her comment, 'take the future baroness to her room for the night.'

'Room?' she challenged, overlooking for the moment his attempt to demote her to baroness. 'It had better be more than just one room.'

The baron had already turned his back, leading his horse by the reins to the stable where he would personally wash him down and tend to his feeding.

Allura clenched her fists, watching him walk away.

'Princess, shall we go?' Rodolfo drew her attention.

'Did you fuck my slave as well?' She whirled to face him. 'Answer me, damn you.'

'No, I did not,' he stated indignantly, looking hurt by the accusation.

'Good, keep it that way,' she said, feeling a little guilty for turning her frustrations on the poor man. But Rodolfo said nothing in response.

A few minutes later he was opening the door to her room at the end of a long, red-carpeted hall lined with suits of armor, no doubt belonging to the baron's pathetic ancestors. 'Will you require anything further?' he asked, preparing to take his leave.

'No,' she said, 'you are dismissed.'

He bowed crisply and left, Allura closed the door behind him, but it was not long before Veeta arrived, her mistress confronting her at once.

'You will tell me everything,' she demanded of the cowering girl. 'All that you did with those pigs.'

Veeta, bruised and bedraggled, fell to her knees. 'Mistress, I did nothing. It was not my fault. They took me for their pleasure in the wagon. There was nothing I could do.'

Allura, shaking with anger, stormed up to the girl and smacked her cheek, the blow reverberated to her own wrist and for a split second she remembered that she, too, had been struck like this, not too long ago by the baron. 'You lying little bitch,' she hissed, covering her sudden discomfort. 'Do you want me to cut out that slut tongue of yours?'

Veeta wept, putting her head to her mistress' feet. 'Please, mistress, I am scared and so uncertain here; do not be unhappy with me. I have no one else but you.'

Allura felt a lump in her throat – the unfamiliar feeling of guilt. 'Stop your sniveling,' she ordered, her anger abating somewhat. 'Do I look like your mother – deserting cow that she was?' It was a cruel dig, given that Saraveeta's family had all been forced into exile following the disgrace of their daughter in court.

'I am a bad girl, mistress,' Veeta wailed. 'Please punish me.'

'I shall request a studded cane,' Allura told her. 'The kind used on male prisoners. I will draw blood, Saraveeta.'

The girl moaned to hear her old name. 'I live to obey,'

she declared.

Allura put a foot down on the girl's neck, her shoes soiled and dusty from the journey. 'You don't know a thing about pain,' she said cryptically. 'Or suffering.' As if Allura were now an expert after a single beating. 'This baron is our enemy.' She pressed with the heel of her shoe. 'Do you understand me? You must try for once in your life to resist.'

'I will, mistress,' she promised.

'Whatever happens, you work for me, you belong to me, is that clear?'

'Yes, mistress.'

'I'm the one who's taken care of you, remember? Without me you'd be dead or whoring in some brothel, servicing ten cocks an hour, not a copper coin to show for it.'

'I-I am grateful, mistress, I swear.' The girl's mouth sought the princess' other shoe, to lick and kiss.

'Do not ever cross me again, Veeta, or I will exercise my prime right of ownership. Do you know what that means?'

'You may torture, maim or kill me as you wish.'

Allura removed her foot from the girl's neck and nudged her side. 'On your back, slave, and lift your hips.'

Veeta assumed the vulnerable position, but after just a few minutes like this, her bottom raised from the floor, she would be begging to rest back down. But Allura would not have to listen to her because Veeta was a slave and she was free. That was the natural order of things. Some were born to stand tall, others to grovel. She was of royal birth and therefore tallest of all.

'You live to be fucked, don't you?' Allura mocked cruelly. 'You have no other function. But remember that every cock that forces itself between your legs or between your lips is an extension of me. You will banish from your mind the thought of any man – the baron especially. When he is fucking you, you will think only of me and my dildo.'

'Yes, mistress.'

'It is possible to do this,' said Allura to her slave. 'To forget a man like Montreico.'

True enough words, thought Allura, but to whom was she addressing them – the slave girl or herself?

'Soon I will be married, Veeta. Can you imagine that? Since we were little girls we awaited that moment when we would have husbands.'

'Yes, mistress.'

Allura commanded her to squeeze her own nipples, multiplying her anguish. 'But you will never have a husband, Veeta. Only masters. Men who need please you not at all.'

'Yes, mistress.'

Allura felt the excitement between her thighs. She had a special treat for her slave tonight, although the first few times Veeta had been required to employ her tongue as a cock she had cried afterwards for hours, making prayers of supplication to the gods in forgiveness for such an immoral act.

'Please me.' Allura lowered herself to the slave's face, lifting her skirts to her waist. She would not remove them in the presence of the slave lest the girl see how she'd been abused at the baron's hands. 'And I want to orgasm,' she warned, 'or the beatings you will receive later will only be even worse.'

The slave licked well, and Allura smiled with satisfaction. 'When I am married to the baron things will change,' she said. 'He will no longer behave so arrogantly, and he will do as I say. For I am to be queen one day, and his life will be in my hands.'

Allura closed her eyes dreamily, and kneaded her breasts through her gown. Could it be right what the baron had said, that she behaved as a brat because she was trying to lure a strong man to come and put her in her place?

'Oh yes, that's it,' she sighed. 'There's a good little slave.' Allura ran her hands through the girl's hair, reveling in her power. 'Keep up the good work and we'll find you a little treat to eat from your bowl. How would that be?'

'Insolent bitch,' thundered a voice, and she felt a hand in her hair, yanking it by the roots. She opened her eyes, crying out with shock and pain, and the next few moments were a blur as the baron dragged her across the room to a heavy wooden chair.

'You are fortunate we have not yet sealed our bond, Allura, or this incident would mark your swift and final fall from grace.'

She was pushed over the back of the chair, her head to the cushion, her bottom displayed to full advantage. 'Montreico, let go of me!' she shrieked.

'Come here, Veeta,' he addressed the slave directly, 'and observe the price of your mistress' earlier disobedience.'

'No,' pleaded Allura, 'do not let her see.'

There was to be no genteel lifting of skirts this time; grasping the back of her bodice the baron ripped apart her dress, tearing the velvet to shreds, and in a matter of violent seconds she was naked.

Veeta gasped to see the evidence of Allura's beating.

'Amazing, isn't it?' The baron ran a hand over the welts, making Allura whimper and squirm. 'Such a seemingly effective punishment, and yet completely ineffective.'

'Ow...' cried Allura, the caresses reawakening the earlier agonies.

'This is mine,' the baron caressed Allura's sex. 'If you ever allow another to touch, fondle or fuck it, you will pay a price you cannot imagine. Is that clear?'

'Yes…' Allura sobbed. 'Yes…'

'Yes, husband,' he amended. 'The practice will do you good.'

'Yes, *husband*.' She tried to dampen the inevitable sarcasm.

'Your body is pledged to me,' he repeated. 'I will share it with no other.'

She wriggled against his fingers, slick and aroused. 'Yes, husband.'

'You'd like to be fucked, wouldn't you?'

'N-no,' she lied, afraid to demean herself in front of the slave.

The baron smacked her with his hand. 'No wife of mine will be permitted to lie.'

Allura groaned, her cheek against the cushion, the blood rushing to her head. 'Yes, I want it, oh, I need it.'

'Well you shan't have it.' He used her hair once more as a handle, lifting her upright. 'What you will have is a little lesson in humility. I want you to crawl to the bed and get on it, facing me, on all fours.'

Tears formed in Allura's eyes, and not merely from the pain in her scalp; what he was about to make her do in front of her slave would mortify her.

'Is there a problem?' He cocked his arm, fully prepared to slap her.

'No, there's no problem.' Allura simply could not fight anymore. She was exhausted, physically and mentally. The man was too big, too strong and too deviant, and he had far too much ability to make her body betray her. By his will he had reduced her to this, winning the battle of clothing, of posture, of obedience.

If only the little bitch did not have to be there to witness her submission. Allura looked down to the floor. The slave

Veeta was, to all intents and purposes, her equal now. Both girls were naked; both were the same age, and both sex objects in the presence of a strong, lustful male. Which would he choose, she wondered, if he could have only one? The thought made her physically ill. The baron could go to the devil and take the little bitch with him.

Allura simpered as the marble pressed against her knees. It was so hard.

'Do not make me wait,' Montreico warned.

She went down the rest of the way, onto her palms, and quickly, anxious to get this over with, she began to crawl.

'Are you a good slave, Veeta?' asked Montreico, as Allura reached her place of shame on the bed.

'I try, master.'

'A good answer,' he approved. 'Come closer.'

Allura felt a sharp stab of jealousy as the dark-haired girl was allowed to take her place, standing directly in front of him, looking up into his eyes.

'Do I frighten you?'

'Yes, master.'

'Why?' he wanted to know, brushing back strands of hair from her brow.

'Because master is strong and very strict.'

'But why be afraid? If you are a good slave you will never fall afoul of me.'

'No slave is perfect, master. There is reason enough for us all to take beatings.'

Montreico's fingers were under her chin as he kissed her. It was full and soft and not harsh, and it made Allura burn inside that it was not her he was kissing like that.

Veeta stood passively, arms at her sides as he finished with her. 'Have you ever been in love, Veeta?' he asked.

'Yes, master.'

Allura thought instantly of the young man Porfino they both so foolishly lusted for, the one over whom her jealousy had flared to unimaginable levels toward her best friend.

'Not me, I have never loved,' he confessed, brushing her nipples with the back of his hand.

The slave shuddered. 'That is too bad, master,' she sighed.

Impertinent slut, thought Allura. He would surely punish her for that, but instead he strayed a finger down to her sex.

'Yes, it is. Tell me, Veeta, how did you become a slave? You were of high birth. You told me this much before.'

Allura tensed. Would Saraveeta use this opportunity to tell the truth, knowing how much the baron hated his fiancée already?

'I was indiscrete,' sighed the slave, parting her legs for him. 'I allowed a boy... liberties.'

'And now you pay the ultimate price for your natural passions. For the rest of your life.'

'It is not so bad, master.' Veeta was gripping handfuls of material on the man's chest. She was a lusty young lady and he was about to find out just how much passion she could unleash.

'Not so bad?' He seemed surprised. 'But a slave girl is beaten, abused and sold at the drop of a hat.'

'But a slave gets attention, master, from men. I like men, master. I like them very much.'

'You little slut!' cried Allura, unable to restrain herself. 'You worthless whore!'

'That will be enough out of you,' snapped Montreico. 'Unless you'd like to be bound and gagged.'

Allura stung under the verbal chastisement, almost as if she'd been whipped. The man was treating her horribly, and yet his words were making her hot and wet, nearly as much as seeing him take full advantage of her slave in front of her eyes as if Veeta were his own.

As good as gagged, she watched as he put a hand to the girl's shoulder, gently urging her down to her knees. With infinite grace and naturalness, and without being told, Veeta opened the man's breeches and took out his erect penis. She began at once to lick it, showing him all the reverence of a god, and Allura hated the girl for paying homage to a man deserving of nothing but contempt.

'Are you watching closely, Allura?' the baron mocked. 'This girl should give you a few lessons.'

'When I am queen,' she spat, forgetting his injunction, 'I will have you flayed alive.'

The baron smiled forgivingly, entranced by the sweet mouth squeezed tight around his cock, the doe-like eyes looking up at him for approval, seeking permission to proceed. 'Yes,' he said throatily in response to Veeta's unasked question, 'take it deep.'

Allura felt the mounting heat between her thighs. She must have relief from this torment; she must have access to the slave's body for herself.

Veeta was an excellent cock-sucker, as it would be so for any female whose life depended on her ability to please men sexually. The baron was large and thick, so wrapping one hand around the base she did her best to encompass the rest. Allura felt a burning weakness in her belly as she imagined that organ piercing her. Would he enforce his marriage rights over her? It was a possibility she hadn't entertained. A man had absolute access to his woman's body under the law, and denial on her part was considered a serious breech, regardless of circumstances. But she was of royal blood. Theirs would be a unique contract, so she would insist on writing the words herself. There would be no sex between them. No physical contact at all. If the man wanted to fuck, he could fuck his bond wenches. His and not hers, for she would get Veeta back in short order.

'You are a magnificent creature,' said the baron affectionately, running his hands through Veeta's long, silky hair, black as a raven's wing.

Allura made a mental note to cut it all off.

'A master could easily be spoiled,' he noted, positioning himself for what looked like his final release.

Allura was now beyond envy; she wanted them both.

'Back,' said the baron, easing her away gently but firmly. Veeta seemed surprised, but moved back on her haunches. Was he going to fuck her?

'What do you know of men, Allura?' Montreico faced his bride to be.

'Am I allowed to speak now?' she replied peevishly.

He was stroking his cock, legs apart, in a stance of arrogant power. 'You will be mine.' He ignored her sarcasm. 'Does that frighten you?'

'You can't handle me,' she bluffed. 'It's you who should be frightened.'

'I will teach you your place,' he predicted.

'And I will teach you.' It was hard to maintain defiance like this, naked, posed on all fours, her bottom still smarting from the beating at the man's hands.

'Do you know the difference between a wife and a slave, Allura?'

She tried, successfully for the moment, to keep her eyes off his penis. 'No, but I'm quite sure you will inform me.'

'A slave has the luxury of many masters and the hope of change should she not like her current one.'

'You will never own me.'

The baron's eyes flashed as he squeezed his cock tightly in his fist, and then he was erupting, Allura's mouth open as she watched the viscous seed land on the marble, a deposit of creamy unguent, Montreico's eyes fixed on her as he came.

And they were still on her as he snapped his fingers, his face expressionless just as it had been during his orgasm. 'Clean,' he ordered, using a standard command for female slaves.

Veeta fell at once to all fours and began to lap at the baron's sperm, and she did not raise her head until it was all gone, and even then she continued licking the marble floor awaiting clearance to stop.

'Look at me,' the baron said to Allura, giving her no quarter to avoid the power of his gaze. 'Can you do that with your slave?'

'Is that what it all comes down to? Your penis?

Another snap of his fingers and Veeta was licking his cock clean, the girl's eyes closed. She was devouring him with real passion, and it was obvious the man's complete domination of her had left her deeply aroused. After a few moments the baron was once more semi-erect.

'Master?' whispered Veeta, her eyes imploring her own consensual violation.

'To my chambers,' he ordered, 'at the end of the hall. You will wait at the foot of the bed, kneeling, head to the floor, ass facing the door. With your fingers you will hold wide your buttocks until I arrive.'

'Yes, master.' She smiled as though he had just offered her a month's voyage to the pleasure islands at the end of the world.

'You will crawl upon all fours.'

'I obey, master.'

Allura wanted to tear out the eyes of the little bitch. A slave should be humble and broken, but Veeta looked so sensuous, so feminine and empowered as she crawled, moving her limbs just so as to inflame the baron's desire. There was little doubt that he would fall upon her as soon as he got to his chambers.

'I would get some sleep if I were you,' the baron advised Allura. 'Tomorrow is our wedding day.'

'Tomorrow?' Allura knelt up, alarmed by the suddenness of it all. 'But there's been no time to plan, to arrange the ceremony, the reception.'

'These matters are not your concern,' he said dismissively. 'All that is required of you is your presence. Good night.' The baron bowed smoothly from the waist and took his leave.

Allura fumed behind him, scrambling for the vase on the carved wooden table, and he had just closed the door when the glass shattered against it, sending shards and water flying everywhere.

It was a futile gesture, a sign of her complete defeat in yet another battle with the man. Exhausted, shaking all over, she collapsed onto the bed, hugging the pillow, curled like an infant, and thankfully sleep came, carrying her far from her real world troubles.

At some time during the night Allura entered into another existence, that of a dream. She was wearing a very long nightgown that fell to her ankles. Her feet were bare and she was completely naked underneath. She was carrying one of her dolls, the one she'd stripped naked to designate her as a slave. She felt like a child, but she was grown, with a woman's body. Ahead of her, directly in front of her was the castle, much bigger and taller than she'd remembered.

She was about to cross the drawbridge, but she was afraid.

'You must go,' said the voice of a crow, hovering in front of her.

'But I don't know what I'll find.'

'You won't find anything,' said the crow, 'except for what is already inside of you.'

Allura looked down at her ankle, which was encircled in iron. 'Why am I shackled?'

'Because you want to be,' the crow replied, having turned into a bearded owl with the face of her father. Now Allura was more afraid to be outside than inside, and so she began to run across the drawbridge. Below her she could hear the snapping crocodiles, and they seemed to be whispering vague threats and criticisms.

'Those are all the things you said that resulted in punishments for the slaves when you were little,' said the owl, which was now nothing but a voice in her head. 'And the crocodiles are the people after they were punished.'

As fast and hard as she ran she was not able to reach the other side. The bridge just seemed to keep on stretching, forever.

'That's because it's a whip.'

'Leave me alone!' She clamped her hands over her ears, not liking how the voice could read her thoughts, and in doing so she dropped the doll, which made her stop, and when she looked down she saw molten fire.

'It's what you wanted for me,' said the voice, and when she turned back there was the baron to remind her of all the times she'd cursed him to the hell of the demons.

'I didn't mean it,' she desperately explained, but he was telling her it was too late, even as he pushed her over the edge.

The crow was there, trying to give her its beak to hold on to, but she was falling too fast. The air stank of sulfur and rotting bodies hung in the air. She saw pieces of soldiers she'd known who had died in battle, a jewel-covered hand that belonged to her mother, who had died at her birth, and the helmeted head of her father.

Once she actually did get hold of the crow's beak, but it shook her off. 'I can't really help this far down,' it said. 'No one can.'

Twice she thought she hit bottom only to fall further, each time with greater intensity. Her nightgown kept getting burned off and replaced, and every time it turned to ash she could see her own skeleton.

Finally she hit bottom, which was soft and soupy.

'Get up,' said a horned demon with the head of a jackal, the bronzed chest of a man and the legs of a goat, 'and suck me.'

'I'm a virgin,' she tried to tell him, but he struck her across the face with the end of his penis, which was a snake.

'You don't have a choice,' he told her. 'You're my wife.'

Allura decided to make the best of it and offered a little kiss. Its eyes were darting and it was dry and scaly and alien. One little touch of her lips and it took advantage, jumping to the back of her mouth. She tried to scream as it went down her throat, filling her.

No sound emerged. Around them black rocks were forming a circle. The moist ground swirled gray like a swamp and more snakes sprouted like tall weeds. One or two pierced her feet like splinters.

'You have to let them come out of your cunt,' explained the horned demon with the jaundice yellow eyes and enormous hooped earrings, as though his words would somehow make sense of the situation.

Allura fell to her knees. 'Have pity on me,' she tried plead.

'Lick my hooves,' ordered the demon.

She put her head to the ground, the stench of the mud making her gag. The demon's cloven hooves were hot to the touch and it pained her to lick them, but there were whips falling on her back now, whips made of snakes that were cutting and nipping at her skin, making her bleed in a thousand places. At last she succumbed, lapping more fiercely. The hooves were hotter now and her tongue sizzled. She tried to withdraw it and could not.

'Ready for your horse cock?' she heard her own voice, and felt something enter her from behind – not in her seething pussy, but in her ass.

'Very dry,' she was saying. 'Let it be very dry.'

Allura did not understand how she could be talking as though she was outside herself, so the crow volunteered to help by flying up her pussy so he could speak to her more directly.

'This is happening because of what you did to Saraveeta,' the crow was able to tell her when it had crawled inside her head. 'You have to be in her old body and hear yourself abusing her.'

'Where is my brain,' Allura wondered, 'now that you're in my head?'

The crow pecked at the back of her eyeball to make a hole to see through. 'It was fed to all your victims. That's the way it works.'

'Take your horse dick like a good girl,' her own self ordered, and the words sent Allura to a new place, under a table at a state dinner. She was wearing a collar and there was an artificial tail thrust into her ass. Every time she moved – she was on all fours – the tail made her come because it was connected to another in her pussy.

Using her nose she smelled for her master, the baron, and putting her head against his boot, she whimpered.

The baron shook her off. 'Make yourself useful, slut.'

Allura crawled from man to man, offering her services to suck them dry. The conversation continued as they mouth-fucked her one by one. They were talking about the kingdom and how to divide it up now that she was no longer a princess but only a pretty little bitch-slut. Her cheeks reddened with shame but she was very horny, too. She wanted the baron to fuck her. She would beg him later, but first she must service all his guests.

For some reason the last man was filled with an enormous amount of spunk, and as much as she kept swallowing there was more. If she didn't swallow that would be enough reason for her to be put to death, so she really didn't wish to fail. But she was going to explode if she didn't stop.

'I disagree,' the man said, reaching down to clamp her nose so she couldn't breathe. 'Leniency on the peasants only breeds indolence. One must rule with iron not silk.'

Semen filled her belly. Semen filled her throat. Semen to drink, and coming out of her pussy. She tried to stem the flow with her hands, but it began to flood the room.

'Disobedient cunt,' called the baron, but soon they were all overcome by the swirling tide. The man gasped and choked as it went above their heads. She alone could breathe. It was like being under the sea and she felt such freedom and joy. A fish swam by and then another, colored ones with brilliant flashing lights like the jewels of her father's scepter.

She was floating, at last in her element, splendidly free and naked. Putting her hands between the legs she laughed, the bubbles reflecting her joy. There was a push, a spasm, and then the form came out of her womb – a new kind of life, not entirely fish or human, but something in between.

'You will be a mother,' it told her, 'to the world. But you will not be queen.'

Allura tried to enquire of her talking pink embryo but it was evolving before her eyes, sprouting wings and growing muscles and flesh, the sexual organs of the male and female both, and a brain stem twice as powerful as the old kind.

Kindly it reached forth and touched with its webbed hand, slender fingered. 'Thank you,' it said, its voice so melodiously sweet it made her want to cry.

'No,' it shook its head, 'no questions.'

A hand slid over Allura's eyes and she was gone from the sea of sperm, gone too from the brimstone world of demons. On her back, instead, she opened her eyes to a normal blue sky, like that of any day in the kingdom.

'I love you,' said Saraveeta, who was above her in the grass, stroking her cheek.

'I love you, too,' Allura heard herself say.

They were lying in the deep green grass and Allura's lips were full and puffy from being kissed. Her chest was heaving and one of her breasts had been pulled from the skimpy protection of her peasant dress. The wet nipple tingled under a light breeze.

'Why did you stop?' she asked softly, wanting the other girl's lips caressing her once more.

'Because I wanted to stop,' said Saraveeta. Allura's old friend climbed astride her and pinned her hands over her head. She wasn't wearing a peasant dress but breeches, boots and a man's peasant shirt.

'Are you...?'

'A man?' Saraveeta finished her thought. 'What do you think?'

She didn't seem like a man. She was lovely, her long

dark hair sweeping her shoulders, her feminine chest rising with delicious arousal.

'I think,' Allura reasoned, 'that we are lovers.'

Saraveeta, ever so much more confident, lovely and powerful without her yoke of servitude, eased her knee between Allura's thighs, making her spread. 'Wrong, Lurie. You're my little slut, nothing more.'

'L-Lurie?' gasped Allura. 'No one has called me that in years.'

Saraveeta ripped the front of the girl's dress to expose her other breast. 'It would make a good slave name for you, don't you think?'

Allura tried to free herself, unsuccessfully.

Saraveeta, who had gotten much stronger all of a sudden, laughed at the princess' anguish. 'I'm only joking,' she said, though she made no move to release her friend from her current state of bondage.

'It's not funny,' said Allura. 'I want to go home.'

'Give me a good reason.' Saraveeta took the fresh breast in her mouth, sucking the nipple to an agonizing point.

Allura moaned. 'B-because I'm asking you.'

Saraveeta licked her lips devilishly. 'Oh no, Lurie, you have to beg.'

'P-please, Saraveeta, let me go?'

'You have to satisfy me first. As a slut.'

'Yes,' she moaned, her helpless heat weighing on her heavily. 'I will be your slut.'

'You must satisfy my horse's cock, my sweet.'

Allura trembled. 'Yes, Saraveeta…'

'Beg for it,' she pressed, biting the girl's nipple.

Allura cried out, 'Please use me, Saraveeta. Fuck me hard.'

'I intend to,' replied Saraveeta, mounting her.

The cock was rigid and cold. Allura pictured the silver

piercing her; like a sword, like a spear, like the weapon that killed her father. Saraveeta fell into a rhythm, like the beating of hooves and Allura saw him, at the head of his army, refusing the protection of his own bodyguards, riding to certain death.

But why?

Fate, whispered the wind. Fate, repeated the thrust of the cock. The pinned Allura began to spasm, coming all over the dildo. What was Saraveeta's pleasure in this? And why hadn't her father kept his life when so much depended on it?

It had to do with the bloodlines, and a break that must come in order for the kingdom to grow in the future. This much she realized as the dream spilled over into a shadowy night.

Take this, Baron Montreico, she reveled in her female climax; take this and learn your real place in the world.

Chapter Six

'Mistress, are you awake?'

Allura opened her eyes. Veeta stood over her, her hair shiny, her eyes and cheeks aglow. She'd even been given a tiny sprig of flowers for her hair.

'Of course I'm not fine,' she snapped. 'I'm being held prisoner by a beast. And why are you looking so cheerful?'

'It is your wedding day, my mistress,' she beamed. 'Why would I not be cheerful?'

Allura sat up. 'Who gave you those clothes?'

'It is the baron's orders. And I am to help prepare you.'

The slave Veeta was wearing a diaphanous gown of light blue, low-cut, revealing her cleavage. Someone had done her hair, as well.

'What is the meaning of this?' Allura demanded of the gold collar around the girl's throat.

'All of the baron's slaves are so collared.' She touched it lightly, as though it were something to be proud of. 'Is it not beautiful, mistress?'

'Has everyone gone mad?' demanded Allura. 'Take that stupid dress off at once. Take it all off!'

Veeta stepped back, a distressed look on her face. 'Mistress, forgive me, but I am under the baron's orders.'

'The baron? The baron?' Allura flew at her, grabbing her by the shoulders. 'Does the whole world revolve around this petty noble? I am crown princess. Do you know what that means?'

Veeta had no chance to defend herself before Allura

ripped off her gown and tore at her hair. The girl was crying, begging, but the princess was beside herself with rage. 'The collar,' she screamed, trying to pull the welded gold circle from her neck. 'Take off that collar.'

'Mistress, it is forged on me!'

It was Rodolfo who pulled the princess off her. 'Princess, have you gone insane?'

'Unhand me, you cretin!'

He held her by the waist, her entire body lifted off the floor. She was twisting and arching her back, wanting a chance to claw him, and neither had intended for them to end up facing each other, her full breasts against his tunic. Nor had they intended for the full and lustful contact of their lips. The naked princess melted at once, all her earlier fury converting into an overwhelming desire to submit.

'No, princess.' He tried in vain to disengage himself, but Allura's legs wrapped around his waist.

'Take me out of here,' she breathed hotly into his ear, 'and I will marry you and make you the prince.'

Rodolfo hesitated for a moment, and sighing deeply he seemed ready to yield – or rather, to be plucked.

'I'm a virgin...' she purred, pressing her crotch against him, offering added incentive.

'No, I cannot.' He pushed her away and tossed her back on the bed.

Defeated and betrayed yet again, Allura turned on the slave. 'You must kill her,' she pointed to the kneeling girl. 'The little bitch has seen our crime.'

Rodolfo dutifully drew his sword, putting it to the throat of the slave.

'Master, please,' Veeta begged softly, her neck angled back most deliciously. 'Take me first; the slave begs to please the man who will kill her.'

'Don't listen to her,' Allura warned. 'It's a trick.'

Rodolfo's forehead beaded with sweat. He looked to the door, to the window and back to the door as though someone might burst in on them at any minute. 'Do it, slut,' he growled at last, pawing at his clothing. 'But be quick about it.'

'Master,' moaned the slave girl, sitting back on her heels.

'You fool!' cried Allura. 'You waste yourself on a filthy slut when I offer you the nectar of the future queen?'

'I need time to think, princess, you must understand. What you ask me to do, it is the worst treason imaginable.'

'Well you haven't any time. The wedding happens today, you idiot!'

Rodolfo grunted, pushing himself to the back of Veeta's mouth. He came immediately, and she drank him down all too happily.

'Look at me,' he demanded when she had finished licking his penis. He put the sword under her chin, drawing a drop of blood at the point. 'If you ever breathe a word of this I will see to it you suffer the most brutal, agonizing death possible. On this you have my word as a huntsman.'

'Yes, master,' whispered the slave, her lips slick with saliva. Rodolfo frowned, but returned the sword to its scabbard, and at once the girl fell to her belly and kissed his feet.

'I must go,' said Rodolfo.

'Good riddance,' the princess hissed, and Veeta remained prostrate as the door closed. Allura despised her all the more for her easy subservience, and a wave of sadistic desire overcame her as she told the girl what they would say to the baron about her dress.

'You will tell him you tried to escape, but I stopped you. You will ask him to torture you severely as punishment.'

'Yes, mistress.'

'Come here so I can give you the appropriate bruises to fit our little story.'

'Yes, mistress.'

'Did I say you could get up first?' She stopped the girl from rising to her knees.

'No, mistress.'

Allura watched her crawling on her front, and just had to slip her hand between her own thighs. 'Go around the room a few times like that, I want to masturbate watching you.'

'Yes, mistress.'

'Who owns you, Veeta?'

'You do, mistress.' She sounded broken, contrite.

'Who will own you always?'

'You, mistress.'

'Good girl. Now come here and we will discuss how I intend to have you kill the baron.'

The wedding ceremony was to be held in the castle's small chapel. The windows were made of colored glass, the designs depicting the story of creation and the exploits of the various gods and goddesses. The seats were of heavy cedar, imported from the great valley of the south. An altar occupied the front, directly beneath a huge mosaic showing the making of the earth from the hand of the sky god, Zuranos, its original form being that of a seed laid upon the fertile womb of the cosmic mother, Hechira.

The priest was the chaplain of the baron's house, as well as the keeper of the shrines in the villages under the baron's tutelage. He was a gaunt, white-bearded man with sunken cheeks and hollowed pockets for eyes. Life seemed to have gone on too long for him and become too tedious.

His fingers were long and gnarled, and he wore a long gray robe stitched with intricate designs of red and blue and gold, the colors of divine intercession. Ordinarily on such a happy occasion there would be flowers; white lilies arrayed about the place and rose petals on the floor, but for today there was only stark gray stone inset with gold candelabras, the equally stony faces of various saints looking down upon them from their rostrums.

The assemblage was equally stark. Representing the family of the bride was the hastily summoned regent, Grand Duke Fortragian, dressed for the occasion in purple velvet, with his gold medallion of office round his neck. On the other side, standing with the baron, was Rodolfo, who would serve as second witness and best man. Otherwise the chamber was empty of guests, having been carefully sealed by the baron's soldiers.

As a virgin the princess wore a gown of white, and the fact that it had to be made so hastily, yet fit her so perfectly was astonishing, and perhaps another piece of evidence that this sham wedding had been planned for some time. Baron Montreico had set her up, she was sure of it.

Allura could not argue the dress's beauty, though. Slung off the right shoulder, gathered tightly about her waist, it was both elegant and sensual. It was crafted from lace, silk and pressed flowers, interwoven to match a brocade in her hair, which was down, combed lustrously over her bare shoulders.

'By the power of Hechira, Mother of the Gods,' declared the priest, summoning first the bride and her escort, 'we invoke the fertility of womanhood.'

The grand duke, stiff and silent, moved arm in arm down the specially carpeted aisle with Allura; not what he'd expected for his grand niece, not by a long shot.

The priest held out a hand, directing them to their place in front of him, slightly to the left, and a young acolyte, perhaps nineteen, wearing a black robe, spread the incense at Allura's sandaled feet. The smell of jasmine and rosewood lifted sweetly to her nostrils, giving momentary hope that something redeeming might come from this travesty.

'By the power of Zuranos, Father of the Gods, we invoke the spell of manhood.'

With this invitation the baron and his best man came forward from the rear of the temple. They wore tunics of black velvet, the baron's decorated with a gold lion upon his chest, the insignia of his house. Silver swords hung at both men's sides.

'The Prayer of Uniting,' called the priest, raising his gray-robed, bony arms when the two men had taken their positions to his left, just across from Allura and her uncle.

Allura heard nothing of the spoken formula, or the priest's adlibbed words to follow. Her mind was essentially blank until she heard him call out that it was time for the consecration. The grand duke kissed her hand, offering a symbolic goodbye, while the best man knelt on one knee and bowed his head before her. Following these signs of homage both men retreated, taking up places well behind the bride and groom.

'Do you,' the priest said to Allura, dispensing with a few more formalities, 'pledge today, yourself, body and soul, without reservation, grievance or hesitancy to this man?'

She looked at him, her mouth dry, the blood pounding in her head. 'I do,' pronounced her lips, quite without the authorization of her paralyzed brain.

'And you,' he turned to the proud and unflappable baron. 'Do you pledge yourself, body and soul, without reservation, grievance or hesitancy to this woman?'

'I do not,' said the baron.

The priest acted as though he had not heard. 'My son?'

'I do not accept,' he pronounced once more, as if it were the most natural thing in the world for him to change his mind with every passing breeze.

Had he not been the one to arrange this service? Had he not been the one to tell everyone he was going to marry Allura?

'I do not understand,' said the priest.

'The matter is simple,' the baron explained. 'This woman comes to me by default of harlotry; she is compensation for a crime.'

'But you agreed to overlook that crime by promising to wed her,' the priest reminded, clearly anxious to return to the script.

'And yet she has not confessed that crime to the gods – not here, at any rate, in the temple of our consecration. I demand that she be made to recount her sins.'

Allura heard the door open and close behind them. Someone else was entering. Out of the corner or her eye she saw Veeta, in a fresh garment of yellow, her hair styled even more prettily than before. She even wore footwear, golden slippers of a fine woven material.

'I demand it,' repeated the baron, his hand resting on his sword.

The priest did not miss the gesture. 'Let it be done as the baron says. The bride will recount her sins, under questioning from the groom.'

Allura remained stone-faced. She would not give the baron or anyone else the glee of seeing her break down on her wedding day. As grossly unfair as this was, she would see the matter through. 'I have nothing to hide,' she said. 'I was tricked by this man into kissing him.'

'The law recognizes no such possibility,' countered the baron. 'Either you kissed me or you did not.'

'I did; and it was the most ghastly experience of my

life.'

'You dishonored my house and yours,' the baron replied, his face expressionless. 'Remove your clothing, young lady.'

Allura laughed, giving the remark the contempt it deserved. 'Are you mad as well as dastardly, Montreico? This is the house of the gods.'

The baron slid his sword from its scabbard. 'That may be so, but I pay the cost of upkeep. Undress, princess, now.'

'Your eminence,' she said to the priest, 'surely you cannot allow this?'

Montreico slashed the hem of the garment, baring Allura's left thigh. 'You will present your naked harlot's body,' he threatened, 'or I will carry out the alternate sentence of death.'

Allura's fingers trembled. 'This is an outrage.' The gown slid from her shoulders to the stone floor.

'All of it, the shoes as well,' he cruelly insisted, and soon Allura was naked, the cool air chilling her skin. 'You will not cover yourself,' commanded the baron, so she lowered her hands to her sides, giving him full visual access to her breasts. 'Your nipples are tight.' He touched one lightly.

'It is the temperature,' she recoiled, resisting the sudden tingle between her thighs.

'Your scent is in the air. It is in your nature to be the seductress, the slut,' the baron accused, and she struck him across the face.

He made no move to hit her back. 'Apologize,' he said simply.

Allura saw the hardness in his eyes, the predatory edge. Here was a man who would make her pay for her insolence, and she imagined the tortures upon her nakedness. 'I... I'm sorry,' she muttered.

'The vows,' said the baron, turning to the equally cowed priest, 'you may proceed with them.' So the priest prompted the baron, allowing him to repeat back the formula. It was time for the ritual lighting of candles, but Montreico had more in mind. 'My bride has more to say,' he announced.

Allura swallowed hard as he turned his attention upon her, full and withering. She wished she could kneel before him to better reflect the inequality between them.

'I, Allura, crown princess of the realm, having disgraced myself and impugned the house and character of Baron Montreico, do accept the following consequences of my actions.' Allura's voice faltered. With each word came the deepening of her sexual need. The man was mastering her, truly.

'Firstly, as the wife of the baron, I accept my subjugation to him in all things. I understand that I must obey him, though I cannot yet fully understand all this will entail. I understand also that I am subject to the baron's discipline. He may spank or paddle my bare behind; he may whip or otherwise strike me with instruments appropriate for a naughty female. Likewise, he may strike my breasts, or any other part of my body so long as no permanent injury results.' Allura's breathing quickened with shameful excitement, but phrase by phrase, pausing for air, she repeated the words. 'I further understand that my liberty may be restricted or curtailed in any way. Though a free woman, I grant to Baron Montreico the right to bind and chain me, to cage and confine me according to his whims. I also accept that my body is his personal property, forfeited not only as wife but as slut, on account of my indiscretions.'

Allura turned to the priest, pleading. 'Eminence, is this

not blasphemy to the ears of the holy ones? He wants me for a slave.'

'The old man will not help you.' The baron pressed his blade to her belly. 'You must deal with me, with this sword of metal, or that other which is made of flesh.'

His cock. The bastard was telling her she must submit to his penis or die. '...I grant to Baron Montreico the right to bind or confine me,' she continued.

'Until death do us part,' he concluded when she had caught up with the recitations, then to the priest he waved his hand. 'Get on with it, if you please.'

The priest nodded hastily, the anguish clearly written on his face. 'Let us pray, bow your heads,' he said to the assembled, 'and close your eyes.'

The baron seized her sex during the prayer, and forced on tiptoes she had to stifle her moans. The priest could hardly have missed what was going on, but he was not about to make a fuss, not with the baron in the mood he was.

'Amen.' He cleared his throat, clearly praying himself for the debacle to come to an end. 'You may kiss one another as man and wife.'

Allura did so reluctantly, afraid of what another kiss would do to her already frazzled nerves, but the baron had something else in mind, and holding her shoulders to keep her back he pressed down. 'You'll be kissing elsewhere, wife.'

His cock. He wanted her to pay homage with her mouth, here, in front of witnesses.

'My lord,' said Rodolfo, 'surely you don't mean to—'

'Do you question me?' the baron snapped, suddenly enraged. 'Do you wish to have your head severed from your body for insolence?'

Rodolfo lowered himself to one knee and bent his head

in a show of obeisance. 'I beg the pardon of my lord,' he said.

Montreico growled, the sword poised to strike the exposed neck of his closest associate, but Allura, reacting instantly to save the man, pressed her lips to Montreico's crotch. He was already semi-hard, a satisfied grunt escaping his throat, announcing the conclusion of the service. 'Get out, all of you,' he snarled, grabbing his bride's hair. 'Anyone entering this chamber in the next hour I will slay with my own hands.'

'But baron,' the priest spoke up at last, 'you cannot desecrate the place of the holy gods.'

The baron's eyes were wild with lust. 'I offer virgin blood, old man, upon the ancient altar.' He laughed darkly. 'What more could you ask for?'

'Come, your eminence.' Rodolfo restrained the old man from rushing upon the baron. 'Let us take our leave.'

'And now, baroness,' Montreico turned his attention to Allura when the others had left, 'it is time you and I got better acquainted, don't you think?'

Allura whimpered at his feet, under his total control, her hair balled in his fist. 'Please, you're hurting me.'

He tightened his grip and bowed her back. 'I like to hurt you, remember? And you're my wife now, so get used to it.'

'W-what are you going to do to me?' She looked up at him in awe.

'Exactly what you expect, my princess of the blood, I am going to fuck you on the holy altar.'

'But why not a bed?' she asked, dismayed.

He reached down for a savage grab of her breast. 'You're soft enough. You'll pad the stone slab for me.'

Her resistance was short-lived. 'Very well, I will do as you say.'

'Indeed you will, for now.'

Again she thought of what he'd said to her on the way to the castle, about how he both expected and wanted her to fight, so he could enjoy breaking her.

'Beg me to fuck you, princess, on the altar.'

Submission hung in the air, mingled with her fast breathing and whimpers of pain. 'Please,' she gasped, 'fuck me… on the altar.'

The baron shoved her back onto her bottom. 'Get up and dance for me, slut. Give me a good reason to be bothered with you.'

Allura rose shakily to her feet, feeling it was not she; not her body but someone else; a young woman flush and ready and wicked in this room; a girl craving domination; a girl who would deny after the fact what was so abundantly clear in the moment.

She knew nothing of dancing, she'd never moved her body in such a way, but she had witnessed the dancing of slaves before. In the days of her father's court, when he was not at war, he was famous for filling the castle with lovely captive wenches who would move beneath the lash, advertising their wares, hips swaying, buttocks and breasts pushed out, their writhing suggesting what else they were good for.

'Show me your cunt,' demanded the baron, his expression giving little away, and Allura opened her legs, gyrating her hips. Could he see the glistening juices coating her tight virginal opening? 'Touch yourself, spread your lips.' Allura obeyed, pinning back the wings of her labia as she swayed. 'Hold your breasts, too.' His commands were forthright and greedy, and she could tell instinctively what she was in for.

'Do… do you think I'm pretty?' she wanted to know, her voice resounding like heresy in the hall of the gods.

'I think you have the body of a slut, Allura. You may pinch your nipples for speaking without permission.'

She did so hard, wanting to feel like a punished slave.

'The pain makes you wetter,' he observed smugly.

Allura moaned, caressing herself. She could not keep her eyes open, she could not keep her body still. 'W-what is happening to me?'

'You are preparing for me,' he told her flatly. 'Now get on the altar.'

She lifted herself onto the cold slab. 'Will you be gentle?' she asked, parting her legs, but the baron merely pulled off his tunic, bearing a hairy chest.

'On the contrary,' he mused, 'I will savage you like an animal.'

She inhaled deeply, his threat like a sword stab to her pussy, as with absolute arrogance the baron opened his breeches. She shivered at the implications. 'I am at your mercy,' she offered her surrender. 'I yield to you.'

He moved to her naked, his body like that of a statue, the thighs of a centaur, his stomach toned, and below it his rigid cock. 'I require no yielding.' He unfastened his raven-winged hair, unfurling it like the flag of some dark and foreboding country. 'I will master you as I see fit.'

'Yes, sir,' she whispered, then bracing herself, palms on the slab beside her, Allura attempted to absorb him. Seizing her ankles he wrenched them wide apart, and she nearly orgasmed from this display of power alone, from being insolently exposed for penetration. 'B-baron,' she whispered, feeling foolish for using his title in such circumstances.

'Speak again and I will beat you,' he warned, and then his cock penetrated her with a single thrust of his hips, and Allura prayed her scream did not constitute a violation of his commandment. It was only part pain; the other elements being wonder and a deep, deep fulfillment. Struggling to obediently suppress her verbal responses she clung to him, his denial of her right to express herself making her feel that much more animal.

'Don't think it escapes me what you're about,' the baron growled, withdrawing to his tip and sinking into her again. 'I know your kind; selfish, ungrateful, the perfect little bitch.' With each invective he treated her to a new assault, making a mockery of her virginity, so long held for her wedding night. 'I will tame you, Allura. You will eat from my hand. You will not merely fear or obey; you will succumb. I will be your god.' She pushed herself against him. He was damning them both. They were fucking on an altar and he was calling himself divine, taking the part of the god of sky to her mother of creation. 'Our children will rule this world, Allura. You will bear me sons. You will be my obedient little brood mare.'

She clawed his back. So that was it; he wanted the world. At last, something to use against him; this and his insecurity, his obvious need to impose upon her his own sense of superiority. These were all the weapons she needed, and the stupid slut Veeta, too. She mustn't forget the slave who would be her dupe, her instrument of death.

'You will never rule anything,' she blurted, wanting to anger him, wanting him to push himself and her over the brink. 'You are a second class noble and always will be.'

The baron roared with his orgasm, the veins on the side of his neck threatening to burst. He had Allura's breasts squeezed so tight in his hands she shrieked with pain as she too reached her blissful climax.

'You'll take it in the ass now,' he panted heavily, seizing control of her hair yet again. 'But I'll let you worship me again first.' Withdrawing, he maneuvered her like a ragdoll to her knees, and Allura could only mumble around the still erect penis that sank into her mouth. He clamped her head with his hands. 'You need to learn discipline. You need a man's control.'

The princess sucked her husband's cock, having little choice but to seek to meet his demands. Was this really happening? Was he really doing this to her in the temple, as part of her own wedding service?

'This is a much better use for your mouth, don't you think, than all that complaining and sarcasm that usually spouts from it?' he sneered, but her only answer was a gurgle, a helpless acknowledgment of his supremacy. 'This is the beauty of the female sex,' he rationalized. 'A woman can be allowed all sorts of freedoms and pretenses of equality, but as soon as the erotic element is added she falls once more into complete subjugation.' The baron's cock was thickening again and she began to wonder if he intended to ejaculate in her mouth.

'During the act of sexual intercourse every female becomes a slave, Allura,' he commented. 'Remember that. It is just that some are allowed to be free afterwards, or at least to appear so.' Allura closed her eyes, but was instantly ordered to open them again. 'Hands behind your neck, interlace your fingers,' he commanded, and she did so, bound now by his will.

'You see?' he noted the excitement in her eyes, 'it is in the blood of the female to surrender, to belong to the male.' He pulled his cock out, glistening and wet. 'Brace yourself over the altar,' he curtly ordered, and Allura did so as best she could, the ancient marble chafing her belly and breasts as the baron's hands clamped her waist, holding her in place. 'Now you will be completely mine...'

Allura winced as he pressed unceremoniously, invading her utterly. 'Take it,' he commanded. 'Take it deep.'

Allura dissolved beneath the onslaught. He was working

himself deeper, possessing her, like she was a part of his property, and as his cock sank deeper and his groin pressed against her buttocks she felt the pain of the welts, making her gasp. She clawed at the lifeless slab, like a gravestone marking the death of her innocence, the end of her freedom.

'The ass is a superior conquest,' he moved back into lecture mode. 'Its penetration has no other value than the man's will and pleasure; it is no reproductive valley, nor is it primarily pleasant for the female. The more enjoyable it is for the male, in fact, the more she is opened and put at his mercy. What about you, Allura? Do you enjoy being plowed?'

'You,' she moaned, the words barely forming in her tight throat, 'and I... are damned.'

'Damned?' he laughed. 'I don't think so, my dear. The gods, if they have any existence outside our brains, respect power. Zuranos is nothing if not a tyrant who takes whatever women he wishes.'

'W-will you come inside me?' she asked, taking advantage of the apparent lifting of the ban on speech.

'Will I fill your ass with my sperm, do you mean?' he goaded. 'More likely on it, then we can rub it in to your flesh, put your clothes back on and march right past my guards and officials waiting outside that door.'

'Why do you hate me so much?' she complained. 'Did I really do you such evil?'

'Personally, no. But consider me the collector for your debts to all the others you've wronged.'

'But I'm just a girl,' she pleaded, all pretense gone.

'And that is how I am treating you. Your slut Veeta is much better at this, by the way.'

Allura tried to keep the images from her mind, of this man, now her husband, stuffing his insolent cock inside the little whore's anus, using her, conquering her. 'I... I need to come,' the princess moaned. 'I need you...'

The baron withdrew his cock. 'You don't deserve it. Kneel in front of me. Beg me to come on your face.'

Allura wept. 'Please, sir... give me this small kindness.'

He delivered a punishing smack to her bottom. 'You will learn to obey me,' he threatened.

Allura sank to her knees, chastised, a lowly punished wife. 'I beg you,' she whispered, her breath ragged, 'to come on my face.'

The baron seized hold of his throbbing cock. 'Look at me.'

Her eyes lifted to his, the reality of her status driven home.

'This,' he grunted, viscous fountain spurting from the eye of his organ as he took malevolent aim, splattering his seed on her fair cheeks, her chin, the tip of her nose, 'is only the beginning.'

That evening, alone in the baron's bedroom chamber, Allura found some paper in his desk and composed a letter to her uncle, outlining her plan for assuming the crown for herself now that she was married. Confidentially, she alluded to him that the baron was controllable, and that he could be sure the kingdom's interests would be safely in her hands.

She closed the letter using the baron's wax and seal, because she did not have her own, and then spent some time pondering ways to smuggle the letter to her uncle. After this she thought of creative ways to kill the baron using one or both of her designated, unwitting agents, the slut Veeta and the dupe Rodolfo.

Still no baron returned, and by now she was quite hungry. The sun was long gone and the moon had taken its place, so knocking on the inside of the door to get the attention of whoever might be guarding the other side, she asked politely for something to eat. Hearing nothing, she asked less politely.

Finally, to silence her cursing, a guard called through the door that she must be quiet and that only the baron was free to release her. Furthermore, if she did not obey this order he would be obliged to come in and punish her himself, a task he did not relish.

The princess blushed crimson at the idea of one of the baron's men laying a hand on her, but at the same time it was a scandalously sexy idea. 'I will not be silenced by a mere servant,' she insisted through the paneled door. 'I am hungry and I want something to eat!'

The door suddenly unlocked and opened, and the guard entered. He was tall and muscular, and his coloring, blond like her, was quite rare among the baron's men. 'Princess, you must stop making such a noise,' he said to her firmly.

Overcome by a strange, lustful fury she challenged, 'Make me.' The guard scowled. 'Go on,' she dared, 'make me. You know you want to. Look at me. I'm beautiful. I'm royalty. Would you prefer to use your hand, or your belt? Are you man enough? Can you make me beg like any other female? Can you make me whimper for forgiveness?'

The man's cock was visibly swollen beneath his uniform breeches, his fists clenched in restraint.

'Go on,' she taunted, knowing she was risking both their fates. 'Show me there's at least one man in this castle besides the baron.'

'Princess, I will deal with you if you don't be quiet,' he said.

'Will you beat me?' she goaded, and with a swift movement he twisted her arm behind her back, making her squeal with shock and not a little trepidation that she'd perhaps gone too far.

'You royals are all crazy,' he muttered, pulling a length of leather twine from his belt, and Allura's wrists were easily secured behind her back. 'You're his slut, not mine.' The guard pushed her forward to the bed. 'Let him deal with you, the gods help him.'

'What will you do with me?' she asked, a little timorously now.

'Tie you up, princess, like the unruly filly you are.'

The princess felt a sudden wave of panic; it was bad enough being left alone hungry and thirsty, but to be in bondage at the same time would make that much worse. 'Wait, please, I'm sorry for being such a bitch,' she said, a little meek now. 'It's just that I haven't eaten for so long.'

The guard gathered Allura's bare ankles together, binding them with another leather strip.

'H-have you a girl?' she asked, finding his powerful presence increasingly attractive.

'There is a wench in the village,' he answered. 'She lays for me when the mood suits me.'

'She belongs to you?' Allura asked.

'She has a husband and children, but I'm the one who knows how to fuck her.'

'And her husband doesn't know?'

The guard laughed, the rough sound of a man used to having his own way. 'Of course he knows, but he also knows to keep his mouth shut unless he wants trouble.'

'You would hurt him?'

He pulled back her ankles rudely, connecting them with a quick tie to her wrists. 'The penalty for defying the baron or his soldiers is death,' he told her.

Allura's heart pounded. She felt so deliciously vulnerable.

'Is... is she pretty, this wench of yours?'

'She has a good body, and she knows how to fuck,' he said, shrugging dismissively.

'As good a body as mine?'

'No,' he answered frankly, 'you are one of the most beautiful females I've ever seen.'

'So why not touch me?'

'Because I like my head attached to my shoulders.'

'But I won't tell.'

'You're a female,' he stated cynically. 'Females always tell in the end.'

'Do you beat her?' Allura wanted to know.

'Beat who?'

'Your woman?'

'If she annoys me, yes. Or sometimes for sport.'

'What do you use?'

'A leather whip,' he stated, and then looked at her quizzically. 'You have a lot of questions about being a lower class slut.'

'Maybe I want to know what it feels like,' she smoldered.

'Then ask your husband, I'm sure he'll be more than happy to show you.'

'My husband is a monster.'

'Your husband is also my lord,' he warned.

'I meant no offense,' she whispered, wishing she could push him just a little further, to the brink of losing his temper and beyond. 'So tell me, where do you make love to your woman?'

'In her husband's barn, most often. I call for her and she makes ready, clearing out a space, closing the door and removing her clothes.'

'She is aroused when you arrive, I'll bet.'

'Yes, I make her wait on all fours, the whip between her teeth. She crawls to me when I appear and lays it at my feet. She then kisses my boots and asks how she can please me.'

'Does she cry out when you whip her?' Allura pressed, breathless.

'I use a gag, or put a bit in her mouth.'

'Oh, yes... that sounds like a good idea...' Allura clenched her thighs against the threat of an impending, embarrassing climax in front of the servant, without even being touched, induced by the bondage and their words. 'What's your name?'

'Tesotoro, princess,' he said. 'Son of Milatoro.'

'Tesotoro,' she whispered.

'And now you have calmed, and I have secured you for the night, I must leave you,' he said. 'I won't gag you if you promise to keep quiet, with no more silly outbursts.'

'Yes, Tesotoro, I promise.' For some inexplicable reason Allura reveled in the sound of his voice on her lips, and for a split second she felt an intense flash of jealousy toward that woman of his.

'Tesotoro?'

He was turning the handle of the door. 'Yes, princess?'

'Will you be out there all night?' she asked.

'Until the baron's return, yes,' he confirmed.

'Oh.' She closed her eyes and almost at once and fell asleep; the idea of the tall warrior being out there watching over her serving as a warming comfort.

When Allura awoke it was light outside. She pulled with her arms and legs and realized she was still tied as Tesotoro had left her. She strained to look around the room, and there was no sign of the baron. Had he been away the whole night? Weakly, she strained at her bonds, and it was then the hunger hit her, much worse than the night before.

'Montreico...' she attempted to call, though it came out a hoarse whisper, and then the door opened. It was him, his gait crooked, indicating he'd had too much to drink.

'Rise and shine my lazy little bride.' He kicked the side of the bed and guffawed, obviously enjoying his own humor at the expense of the helplessly bound girl. 'Then again, I suppose you can't very well rise, can you?'

'Where have you been, Montreico?' she demanded.

The baron frowned and took a swig from the ale flagon he was holding. 'By the gods, woman, not even twenty-four hours married and already you're nagging me.' He roared with laughter again, the raucousness of which required him to support himself upon the nearest bedpost.

'I am glad you are amused, *husband*,' she snapped. 'But I am starving and cramped and thirsty and I must go to the bathroom.'

Montreico slumped down beside her on the bed and slapped her nearest thigh. 'Yes, sorry about that, I'm afraid we got a bit carried away in our celebrations last night.'

'Celebrations? Of what?' she asked.

'Why, my marriage, of course. You should have been there, it was quite a feast.'

Allura clenched her fists. 'Are you telling me while I lay up here alone, trussed up like a roasting pig, you were feasting and drinking?'

'And whoring,' he added with a deep sigh. 'Don't forget the whoring.'

Her predicament forgotten for the moment she said, 'And you dare to tell me that my body will be your property and yet you give yourself to sluts?'

'I'm a man,' he said simplistically, clearly believing that to be justification enough. 'Look, if you're just going to nag me I'll leave you to stew in your own juices a few more hours.'

'Wait,' she cried as he rose, 'don't leave me. Please, I can't be left like this any longer.'

'And I can no longer bear the company of a spoilt little bitch, Allura. Are you prepared to apologize?'

She was all set to voice her indignation, but she knew it would only lead to more pugnacious behavior on his part. 'I... I apologize,' said the once haughty princess.

'For being a spoilt little bitch?' he pressed.

'Yes,' she replied, tears in her eyes. 'For being a... a spoilt little bitch.' But how the words stuck in her throat. Was it being a spoilt little bitch to request such simple considerations?

'And you are prepared to be a good little wife?' he prodded, downing another swig from the flagon.

'Yes,' she shamed herself all the more deeply, 'I am prepared to be a good wife.'

'And to obey?'

'Yes.'

He laughed. 'As long as I have you over a barrel, at least.'

'Wait, where are you going?' she asked, as he staggered to his feet and weaved slightly towards the door.

'I need a few things,' he said, belching, 'to continue your lessons.'

Allura shivered at the implications. She did not want lessons, she wanted to eat, drink, and the ablutions. He left the door open behind him and with every passing second her heart sank further and further. For so long she had tried to be strong, but the tears were welling up.

'Montreico,' she whimpered, sobbing slightly at his eventual return.

'Miss me?' he grinned, and she almost had, pathetic though that felt.

'What is she doing here?' Allura demanded, seeing the slave following him in.

'Saraveeta has brought your breakfast,' explained the baron.

Allura stared vehemently at the slave, her short silk tunic complimenting her curves. 'That is not her name, Montreico,' she said.

'It is now. I've changed it back.' The baron snapped his fingers and Saraveeta lowered to the floor the tray she was carrying. On it were two bowls, one containing water, the other filled with a gray, pasty substance.

'That had better be hers,' commented Allura.

'These?' The baron looked innocently at the dog feeding vessels. 'No, Saraveeta has already dined. Haven't you, my dear?'

The slave lowered her head; her cheeks blushed as Montreico rubbed his crotch suggestively.

'I must use the toilet,' said Allura, deciding to ignore his goading, for the moment.

'Certainly,' he said. 'Saraveeta, fetch the chamber-pot.'

'Put it there,' he pointed as she presented it. 'On the floor.'

Allura sputtered. 'You can't expect me to…'

The baron cut the binding straps on her wrists and ankles. 'Unless you'd like to go on the floor?'

'You will at least leave the room,' Allura said indignantly.

'No, why would I do that?' he taunted, ordering Saraveeta to help her to the iron pot on the floor. 'I will watch. It pleases me to do so.'

'I will not squat for you like a bitch, Montreico,' Allura vowed, feeling lightheaded from her lack of food or drink as she struggled to her feet. 'Don't touch me,' she said petulantly as her former friend tried to assist her.

'A wife hides nothing from her husband,' he stated

pompously. 'You will piss in front of me or not at all.'

'Fine, then I'll wet your bed,' she said petulantly.

Montreico wagged an unsteady finger. 'That sort of childish display will earn you a stiff beating, my dear. One that will make it difficult for you to sit for the next week.'

'What are you looking at?' Allura snapped at the hovering Saraveeta, who seemed to have no reason to be present but to make trouble.

The girl dropped to her knees. 'Nothing, mistress,' she cowed before the princess' outburst. 'I meant no offense.'

'Well you did offend me, you stupid whore.'

'Allura, I will not permit you to speak so to my slaves.'

'*Your* slaves?' she gasped.

'Yes, my slaves. Among whom is this one, Saraveeta, who is owed an apology by you.'

Instead of apologizing she struck the girl. 'How's that, Montreico?'

By way of an answer the baron spoke calmly, sounding suddenly sober. 'Saraveeta, go to my closet. In it you will find instruments of discipline. You will bring me the leather whip.'

'You're bluffing,' said Allura. 'Even you wouldn't dare use such an instrument on a princess of the blood.'

A few moments later he was wielding it, sleek and black like a venomous snake. When he cracked it, expertly, the blood drained from Allura's face as she saw the determination in his expression; not only would he use the lethal implement, he would take delight in doing so.

'Montreico, I see no cause for conflict here,' she said quickly, backtracking. 'Surely we can reach an arrangement.'

'The only "arrangement" that interests me, princess,' he snapped the tip of the dastardly device an inch from her face, 'is to have you writhing on the floor, helpless to avoid your inevitable punishment.'

'Baron,' she put out her hands, 'give me another chance. Let me please you.'

'You will, Allura,' he vowed confidently, 'you will.'

The first blow struck her exposed stomach, searing the taut white flesh, and the princess cried out, looking down at the vicious red line.

'Now that I have your attention, my dear, I'd like you kneeling before me, where you belong.'

Allura slid to her knees, humbling herself. 'Please,' she cowered, but he took a slice at her thigh.

'Were you given permission to cover yourself?' he demanded.

'But the pain,' she complained.

'Pain?' he scoffed. 'What do you know of pain? I'm quite sure you give ten times this much to your slaves. To Saraveeta, for example.'

Allura sought to shuffle back out of range, her dignity quickly evaporating, but he easily lashed her ass, then another blow across her shoulders brought her down onto her front.

'You have a lot to learn, my dear. Your every defiance brings you more suffering.'

The princess no longer attempted to move. She took the next two blows with whimpers, one to her upper thighs the other again across her shoulders, a fine sheen of sweat forming on her agonized flesh.

'You look very fetching this way, Allura,' he continued to mock her. 'Shall I describe the marks to you?

She cringed, not knowing if she was expected to answer or endure in silence.

'Crawl to me, wife,' said the baron. 'And don't bother getting on your hands and knees; your belly will do fine.'

Allura slithered across the cold floor, well aware that her own slave was witnessing her disgrace.

'You may kiss them,' he said, when she reached his boots. She stiffened in silent rage, but dared not disobey.

'You obey well,' he mused, as she delivered tiny kisses with trembling red lips. 'Perhaps I shall have you do this for all my men.'

He saw the shaking of her indignation and laughed. 'Relax, princess, we do have to maintain your station. You'll be my slut and no one else's.'

Allura felt the seconds burn like hours. She was dizzy, and not only from hunger or thirst or shame.

As if sensing her simmering needs, he probed her verbally. 'What are you prepared to do now, Allura?'

'I will do what you say,' she breathed between kisses, wanting him to push her hard. 'I will obey.'

'But you've already been given instructions, haven't you? And you chose to ignore them.'

'Yes,' she acknowledged, 'I failed to obey.'

'What will you do to fix it?'

'I will urinate,' said the princess, on the verge of yet another shameful orgasm, 'as I was told to, in the pot.'

'And afterwards?'

'I… I will do whatever I am told next.'

'You will take your breakfast,' he supplied. 'You will crawl on all fours to the bowls I have so graciously set out and you will feed.' He pushed her away with his boot.

'How does this make you feel?' the baron asked, some minutes later, choosing the most damnable time to ask.

'I feel… humiliated,' she replied, squatting over the chamber-pot, her urine tinkling into it. 'It's not fair to treat me like this.'

'I decided what's fair in your life from now on, Allura,' he pointed out. 'If you want to eat you will do as I've told you.'

The shame was overwhelming, being forced to perform such a private act in front of him, and worse, her slave, but eventually her bladder was empty and she could at last eat.

'Saraveeta,' the baron said, his tone mischievous, 'does your mistress ever require you to behave like an animal?'

'Yes, master,' the slave answered honestly.

'You feed from bowls?'

'Or else she tosses me scraps on the floor, master.'

'Your mistress is very cruel to you, is she not?' he continued, like some judge in court.

'I am a slave,' she answered expeditiously. 'Mine is not to judge.'

'But you were once friends. Isn't that so?'

The pretty slave squirmed, fearful she might incriminate herself. 'Yes.'

'And now your friend owns you. Quite a turn of events, wouldn't you say?'

Saraveeta's eyes darted nervously to her mistress, but Allura was in no position to interfere anymore. 'It was a great turn, yes... but all was by law,' she added quickly.

'Yes, I've looked into the matter for myself,' the baron mused. 'You were accused of harlotry with a boy your own age at court. His name was Porfino.'

Saraveeta's eyes lowered, and she made no comment.

'Were you guilty?' he asked the dreaded question. 'Did you give yourself sexually to this boy?'

'Yes, master,' she replied.

The baron's dreaded sword emerged, skillfully slicing the air. 'The penalty for lying to one's master is death,' he reminded her. 'And in your case, if you are not honest with me I shall cut you open from groin to breast. So once again I ask, were you guilty?'

Saraveeta fought back a sob. 'N-no,' she said, her voice barely audible.

'Speak up, I can't hear you.'

'No, master, I was not guilty.'

'But there were witnesses.'

'Only one, master.'

'Only one?' The baron acted surprised. 'And who might that be?'

'The princess, master.'

He put a hand to his brow in mock surprise. 'The princess?'

'Yes, master,' she replied, maintaining her level tone despite his sarcasm.

'I am shocked,' the baron sighed. 'Allura, is this true? Never mind, you may take a drink. We'll take this up later.'

Her pride shattered, Allura slurped gratefully and noisily at the bowl of cool water, gulping it down, quenching her intense thirst.

'Slow down,' he advised, 'you'll choke.'

When she looked up a few seconds later the water was gone.

'Now you may feed,' the baron allowed, and as disgusting as the gruel looked and tasted, she was way past being fussy and swallowed it down without bothering to waste time chewing.

'So you were falsely accused,' the baron mused, turning back to Saraveeta. 'You never touched this Porfino?'

Saraveeta shook her head sorrowfully.

'Didn't you like him, then?'

'I did. I loved him, master.'

'But he did not love you?'

'Begging your pardon, master, but he did.'

'But he rejected you. He could have married you and

spared you this slavery. Why did he not do that?'

'Th-there was another,' she said hesitantly.

'Another?'

'Yes, master. Porfino loved the princess. He went to her, throwing me aside with her encouragement.'

'But she did not marry him.'

'No.' Saraveeta paused, as if she did not wish to say the rest. 'She cast him aside.'

'That must have been hard on him.'

'Master, Porfino killed himself,' said the slave with surprisingly little emotion. 'Just a month afterward.'

Allura's mouth froze in the bowl.

'For love of our dear Allura,' the baron offered dramatically, the sarcasm evident.

'That is a lie,' cried the princess, lifting her face, her mouth caked with gruel. 'Porfino died in battle. He was a soldier.'

'Is this true, Saraveeta?'

'Yes, master, he was a soldier, and it was reported by his commander that he died in combat, but in truth he fell upon his own sword on the eve of battle. He did so out of grief, having just received word from the princess that she did not consider him worthy to marry her.'

'But how could you, a mere slave, learn such a thing?'

'A guard told me this, a veteran, who witnessed it all. He took pity on me one night as I was being used by his company.'

'This usage being one of Allura's punishments for you, I imagine.'

'My mistress likes me to be abused by men as often as possible,' she acknowledged. 'And beaten.'

'And would you like revenge?'

'Master?'

'It is possible, you know, if I allow it. In fact, I could

command it. Allura,' he snapped his fingers, 'crawl over here and lie on your back, legs apart.'

The princess did as she was told, tearing herself away from the sustenance she needed so badly, and taking advantage of her vulnerability the baron inserted the heel of his left boot in her sex. She was warm and wet for him, and with just a little movement to and fro he had her moaning and writhing.

'Why do you hate men?' the baron asked his wife.

'I... I don't know,' she said piteously. She'd meant to say she didn't, only him, but it was becoming ever more difficult under the circumstances to form her thoughts.

'Sure you do,' he countered. 'And it has nothing to do with your past lack of attention from your father, never knowing your mother or any such nonsense. You are the way you are because you have too much freedom. You despise all men because none has stepped forward to give you what you need. Control. Subjugation. Complete and absolute rule of your mind and body.

'That is why you have taken Saraveeta into this lonely hell of yours. First you denied her true love, then you forced upon her the unspeakable frustrations of being owned by another female. But you also enjoy empathizing with her, and so you live through her, whenever you send her to be used by men.'

Allura rolled her head from side to side. He'd invaded her mind as perfectly and infuriatingly as he had her sex. 'I don't know,' she gasped, 'what you're talking about.'

The baron pressed his boot, subjugating her cunt. 'You do know and I am here to stop you from lying to yourself.'

She pushed her pelvis up against him. 'Let me come,' she pleaded; ready to take for herself this most disgraceful, humiliating orgasm.

'No.' He withdrew his boot and put it to her mouth to

lick, and the taste of her juices mixed with leather made her swoon. If only she could use her hands on herself. If only he'd let her.

'Orgasms have to be earned, Allura,' he stated. 'I will decide when you have them and when you don't. Just as I will decide what happens to you every moment of your life. Get used to this,' he advised. 'It is how I intend to live. Outside this chamber people will see you a certain way. You will have your aura, your façade, but you will know always, every time you look in my eye, that behind these doors I can and will do anything to you I wish, just as if you were my bond slave.'

The freshly licked boot descended onto her belly. 'You are beneath me,' he declared, 'but you have only scratched the surface of your submission. As I said before, I intend to break you very, very slowly. I apologize in advance for the inconvenience of the cruelty you will endure; unfortunately you have the misfortune to marry a man who is a bit of a sadist – physical and psychological.'

Allura tried to see beyond her need to orgasm. There was so much at stake and she could not afford to give in so easily at this juncture. But he had worked her to a fever and there was no turning back. 'I need to come,' she reiterated.

'We all have needs, Allura. Seldom are they met.'

She blinked back tears, a wave of sentimentality and loneliness overcoming her. Was she really making up for something lost early in life, in spite of what he said?

'Montreico, please,' she pleaded, 'let me be alone with you; make love to me, as your wife.'

His expression grew dark. 'We consummated already, or have you forgotten?'

'No, I have not, but there is more. I feel more. I need more.'

'You need a good hard fuck like the little slut you are, Allura. I'll arrange it for you, but you may not like the results.'

In a terrible gesture of vulnerability she lifted her arms. In front of Saraveeta, no less, she was ready to expose something she'd never known was there. It was not a long-term change, not an answer to anything, but it was in the now and she must rise to this occasion. 'Montreico, fuck me, please.'

He beheld her, his face belying complex emotions. 'No,' he refused, 'I leave that to Saraveeta.'

'Master?' asked the slave, voicing her lack of comprehension.

'The horse dick, Saraveeta,' he elaborated. 'You will strap it on and use it to fuck your mistress. Give her all the orgasms she wishes, but make sure she takes them as a whore, without dignity, begging and humping like an animal.'

Saraveeta was shocked. 'But master, I—'

'Do you seek to disobey me?' he interrupted.

She lowered her eyes. 'No, master,' she replied softly, and Allura noted the ease in their conversation with one another. Was there a bond forming between them?

'Montreico,' she shot back, retracting her foolish emotionalism of a moment before, 'are you so little of a man that you leave a slave girl to do your duty? Fine, I'll enjoy it more with her.' she tormented him.

He smiled slyly, like he could not care less, and then surprised her by leaving the room.

'Veeta, I command you to help me escape,' said Allura, in a desperate attempt to regain some semblance of control.

'The master would not like that,' Veeta said, shaking her head.

'But how can you give loyalty to him? Who has known you all these years, since childhood? Who's been the one to…' Allura's voice trailed off as she realized the foolishness and hypocrisy of what she was saying. They were silent for a few moments, and then Veeta spoke.

'Are you quite finished?' the slave wanted to know. 'Because I think it's high time we got started.'

'Veeta, what are you going to do?'

'It's Saraveeta,' she said, her tone taking on the same intensity of the baron's. 'And you know very well what I am going to do.'

Allura yielded to the stark reality. 'Saraveeta, I beg you,' she sobbed, 'don't do this to me. I'm so, so sorry for all of it. And I'll make it up to you, I swear. But I'm a princess, you can't hold me to the same standards.'

'And what standards are those, Allura? The standards of honor and loyalty and friendship?'

'You are my friend. You are.'

'Go and get the shaft,' said Saraveeta coldly, 'before I become angry.'

The princess' mind looked for angles, for some way to bargain. Could it really be true that she deserved this? 'Saraveeta, I will free you if you let me go,' she offered meekly.

'Do you really think you still own me?' the girl queried, and the princess glared in shock. The possibility that she'd already lost Veeta for good had truly not occurred to her. 'The dildo in your trunk,' Saraveeta reminded, 'I am waiting for it.'

Allura fetched the dreaded silver horse cock and belt.

'Put it on me,' commanded her former slave.

Allura's fingers trembled. It seemed ten times bigger now. 'Saraveeta, I could pay you in gold and diamonds.'

'Pay me?' the former servant scoffed. Is this what our

old friendship means to you? I think you had better shut your mouth before you dig an even bigger hole for yourself. Better still, get on your knees; let's give you a little taste of what's in store.

Allura sobbed, kneeling before the intimidating shaft, upturned and wicked, like a sword from the desert tribes, the forged balls permanently and brutally hard.

'How is it?' Saraveeta wanted to know, as Allura touched her tongue to the metal. 'Is it cold? Just wait till it's in your cunt and ass.'

'M-my ass?' Allura stammered.

'Yes,' she confirmed, 'your ass.'

'But it will rip me,' Allura protested.

'Not if you relax and think about what a little slut you are, and how you need it more than you'll admit. Then it will penetrate with ease. Trust me, I know.'

Allura licked the shaft. Her pussy was on fire, but what she needed was the baron, not what was in front of her.

'You look good that way, Allura,' Veeta mocked. 'I always thought you would. The baron's probably right; you only act like such a bitch because you need someone to master you. All in all I could almost forgive you. Almost.'

The thinly veiled threat induced Allura to suck with more enthusiasm. If she could appease the girl now she might more easily be dealt with later.

'Lubricate it well,' Saraveeta threw her own words back in her face. 'It's going to be awful tight in your ass otherwise.'

The princess whimpered, taking as much of the dreaded phallus in her mouth as she could, desperate to get the ordeal over with.

'You will thank me for the practice,' Veeta teased. 'The baron is also well endowed and rather exacting. You've gotten off easily so far. I've already taken a beating for sucking him not as he wished.'

Allura's insides wrenched at the thought of the two of them together, but why should that specter upset her?

'You have to learn not to gag,' instructed Saraveeta. 'Men will beat you for that. They will expect you to take it all the way to the back of your throat without complaint. Like this...' She pressed on the back of Allura's head, forcing the dildo deep.

'Don't panic,' she coaxed, 'you can take it... your mouth is made for sucking a cock.' Allura sucked obediently. 'Good girl,' Saraveeta praised, stroking her head.

The princess cringed at the patronizing praise, and vowed, never would she sink to this level again.

'You know, Allura,' Saraveeta continued, idly stroking her hair, 'I never did have a chance to tell you what happened to me after my arrest. The guards who took me into custody fucked me, of course, as did the jailor and his assistant. And why not? I was already a whore in the eyes of the law, but the ironic thing is that it was actually the first of the soldiers who took my virginity, and not Porfino as everyone assumed.

'Yes, princess, my maidenhead bled upon the cold, dirty, stone floor of the dungeon. They beat me for my ignorance, my terror of taking a cock in my mouth and for the inaccessibility of my asshole. They'd expected me to be as good as an experienced whore and as loose. But it was my youth and beauty that saved me, or so I was told. Plucking such a flower, rare and highborn, was a great novelty for these men. I do not recall sleeping those first few nights. Mostly I remember the cocks, the endless parade of them and the feet, nudging my exhausted body back to consciousness, the men indifferently and callously ordering me into whatever position they wanted.

'Can you imagine, Allura, barely eighteen and having them come for you again and again. And the whips. Always the whips. Whips if you're too slow, whips if you're too hasty, whips if you appear to eager, whips if you just lay there like a piece of meat. Whips, just because it makes them hard and gets them off.

'For three days I was punished this way, princess. I was allowed to see no one, nor did I ever rise above my knees the whole time. They kept me naked, on the damp floor, a chain of heavy iron around my ankle. Mostly it was dark. I had to feel for the cocks, or else just brace myself as best I could. Lots of them enjoyed ejaculating on me, and lacking any way to clean myself I soon felt and smelled like a cesspool for male sperm.

'This was supposed to help me understand who I was and what I had become. I was not allowed to see my family, until the fourth day. They made no effort to make me presentable. When my father saw me through the bars he howled in rage. My mother screamed and fainted, and my brother had to be restrained from attacking the guards. They were given no chance to speak to me, and I had no voice left for them. I cannot imagine a more horrible thing for them to see, nor will I ever understand how they found the strength to endure my eventual sentencing.

'Some time later my parents spirited my brother from the country so he would not take revenge for you, thereby sealing his own death. They were not exiled, nor did they run away out of shame as the rumors reported. They simply could not bear to lose two children – the loss of one being hard enough. I am dead to them, as is the kingdom. Ours is no nation of sovereignty anymore. It is a place of shame. A harboring place for jackals; men too strong and devious to be controlled by your uncle, and the gods forbid a little monster like you ever sits on the throne.'

Saraveeta made Allura get up and go to the bed, and then ordering her onto all fours she pressed the artificial cock to the tightly puckered entrance to her bottom. 'And now,' she thrust with a deep sigh, 'it is time to finish the story. We're almost to the part where you come in as my gracious rescuer, buying me for a handful of silver coins, but first you shall hear about my last visit from Porfino and the events which led up to his suicide.'

Allura shivered almost as much at the mention of suicide as she did at the feel of the cock pushing into her vulnerable rear passage. Once again Saraveeta advised her to open herself as much as possible, and to listen carefully.

'When I heard Porfino was coming to see me I was beside myself with joy,' Veeta went on. 'At last, I thought, was my chance to escape the terrible fate awaiting me. He looked to me more handsome than ever, his red hair brushed neatly over as he tried to assume the presence of a much older and more responsible man. He wore a green cloak and suit, with the emblem of his family. My heart nearly stopped at the sight of him, even with those unfamiliar worry lines etched into his beautiful young face – a result, I could only assume, of the scandal. Even as the offended party he still had a burden upon him, and there would always be those among the most conservative elements of society who would hold him guilty too, no matter what I had done.

'When he asked to be allowed to come to my cell to speak to me alone, I was sure he intended to make things right with me. At the very least it spelled an opportunity for me to make my case, to plead with him to seal the union I know we both wanted so badly.

'"You do not look well," said I to him, though I must

have looked a hundred times worse, barefoot, my ankles shackled, my hair a rat's nest, my only garment a hastily provided tunic of rough, homespun material that hung barely to my thighs and cleaved deeply between my breasts.

"'It has been difficult,' he replied curtly, and I became at this point very frightened that I had lost him.

"'I have missed you so much,' I shared, pressing my body to his.

"'Do not,' he pushed me away. 'I cannot allow you to dishonor me further.' I asked what he could possibly mean. He of all people should know I had never touched him in any way, other than with my whispered confessions of love.

"'I have spoken with the princess,' said he to me.'

Allura dropped her face to the bed, trying to absorb the impact of what she was hearing, reeling in anticipation of what she knew Saraveeta was going to reveal: her own lies coming home to roost.

'I didn't know what he meant at first, and I couldn't imagine that you would do me anymore harm than you already had. And trust me, princess, in my imprisonment nothing caused me more anguish than trying to figure out what I had done to deserve your betrayal in the first place. But soon I realized you had only just begun your evil plans by denouncing me to the authorities. Your next move was to poison Porfino against me. How did you manage that, Allura? Did you weep in front of him, pretending it was hard to reveal such terrible things about me? He certainly bought your act, though, didn't he? And your lies.

"'You are a whore, Saraveeta,' he accused bitterly. 'With everyone but me, it seems.' And so I was regaled with tales of men I had kissed, and how I had supposedly gone down on my knees to take one of the stable boys in my mouth. You even told him, as I recall, that I liked the game of horsy; being forced to all fours, naked, and subjected to a bridle and bit and saddle, then lathered down, my skin oily and sweat-soaked, I would let them whip me, forcing me to prance and perform. Quite a tale, don't you think, princess? I often wondered where you got that from. Did you see such a thing or was it one of your own fantasies?'

Allura, now fully impaled by the artificial penis, was in no position to obfuscate or delay. Saraveeta could hurt her now, and hurt her badly. 'Yes, I dreamed it,' she said, 'in my fantasies.'

'Did it get you hot?'

'Yes,' Allura confessed, unwittingly pushing her bottom up for even deeper penetration. 'I masturbated thinking of it.'

'And of me, suffering, did that excite you too?'

'Saraveeta,' she moaned miserably, 'you must believe me, I am sorry.'

'It excited Porfino, that's for sure,' Saraveeta ignored the apology. 'Much as he came to condemn me, he was horny as a satyr, too.

'"Is it true?" he wanted to know, licking his lips, and I told him yes, I was just that kind of a whore. What did it matter anymore? I was already guilty, marked for abuse and punishment and sexual servitude for life.

'"You wounded me," Porfino confided, and suddenly he was willing to have my body close to his again. "I could never marry you now; my plans are all upset. Don't you think you owe me something for that?"

'His hands clasped my welted, bruised ass, and I cried out involuntarily as he worked the skimpy garment up to my waist. "You've been whipped," he said, feeling with his hands. Just a few short days before he would have said such a thing with outrage and indignation. But now, thanks to my so-called crimes, he was sounding pleased, if not downright exuberant. I whined that he was wounding me in turn, but he was no longer listening.

'"Do you know how long I've dreamed about this moment?" he asked huskily. "And now it's here I can do whatever I want to you."

'It seemed to elude him that I might have the right to grant or deny permission. All he saw was a semi-naked girl, locked in irons, on the verge of slavery, so having few cards to play with I went right for my ace.

'"Porfino, if you marry me we can be together always, and I can serve you, humbly, till I die." But again he ignored me, devouring my throat as he began to feel me roughly all over.

'"You are so lovely, Saraveeta," he panted. "You drive me mad. I want to make love to you." I pointed out one could never make love in such a place, that I was a prisoner and he was intending to fuck me, nothing more, but I had no power to stop his hands roaming up under my short tunic to my exposed sex. His fingers found easy access to me and as he fumbled I began to moan and rock on them.

'"I can't wait," Porfino croaked, and I found myself pushed to the wall, my knees parted by his hips. He rutted and humped, filling me with his seed in seconds, leaving me agonizingly on the brink.

'"More," I moaned. "More, please." But Porfino was angry now and called me a slut. He made me kneel and clean his penis while he told me of his plans with you. You were going to marry him. You were going to make him king. Did you really say all that or was the poor boy deluded?'

'I... I did say some of it,' Allura confessed breathlessly.

'But mostly I just made allusions and he jumped to conclusions.'

The princess winced as Saraveeta plugged her another inch or so. 'You must have been so proud of yourself,' she sneered.

'I was young then... I was very young.'

Saraveeta laughed sarcastically. 'It was last year, princess. How much changes in a year?'

'Everything, for some people.'

'As if you knew anything about that. For Porfino, yes, everything changed. He abused his true love in a prison cell; he wounded her heart fatally and lowered himself to the level of being just one more assailant, and the guilt punished him till he could bear to live no longer. I said before he received word that same night that you would not marry him, but you and I both know that was only the superficial cause. He was already dead, thanks to you, and he was finishing the job, just as you killed me when you separated us.'

'I-I can't be responsible for all that,' Allura cried. 'I can't handle so much.'

'I'm not surprised, my little pet. You haven't the backbone or the will. Honestly, princess, you had better give some careful consideration as to what you will do with this crown you are working so hard to win. You may have your father's blood, but not his mettle or his wisdom.'

'Saraveeta,' whispered the princess, unable to deny her passions, 'will you fuck my pussy now?'

'Only if you beg,' Saraveeta provoked.

'I do,' Allura gasped. 'I beg you.'

Saraveeta pulled out of her tight rear passage. 'Make me.' Allura reached back for the artificial cock, only to have her arm twisted up behind her back by the other girl. 'You always were the weaker one,' said Saraveeta.

'We are all weak in comparison to men,' Allura countered, then squealed as Saraveeta abruptly plunged the cock into her pussy, pinning her to the bed.

'So you're an expert now?' she mocked.

'It is true,' Allura mumbled against the bedcovers, 'the baron says every woman is a slave during sex. It is only that some are allowed to be free afterwards.'

'A subtle but significant difference, don't you think?' She pumped in and out, establishing a rhythm. 'When you send me to the guards I am used all night long and then must return to comb your hair or draw you a bath. And if I fail to please you on account of being utterly exhausted and aching from head to toe, you will have me sent to the dungeon to lie in darkness, naked and in chains.'

'But we all dream of men,' said Allura boldly. 'We cannot live without their strength. That makes us sisters still.'

'What do you know of my dreams?' The dildo sank deep enough to make the princess whimper. 'What right have you to speak for me?'

'None, none,' she pleaded. 'I didn't mean it.'

'You royal bitches do that all the time. You use our feminine needs as an excuse to brutalize us.'

'But we are of the same class. We grew up together; have you forgotten?'

'No, it is you who has forgotten. And as far as that goes, you never knew in the first place. Did it even occur to you how it felt to always play second fiddle to you, and how it was for my family having to bow and scrape to your father?'

'I knew that, I did. But I could do nothing. Once I asked my father why you could not ride with us in the state carriage to greet the visiting King of Fristia. Do you remember? We were six. He told me I had a good heart but I must learn the way of things. Life was about power. There are those who have it and those who don't, and ultimately all must yield and be slaves to their betters. "Only kings and queens have no betters," he said. "Only they are masters. Your little friend, beauty that she is, will one day have to know herself your slave." Do you know how it hurt me to hear him say such things? I was never so disappointed.'

'So your father was not the hero we thought,' Saraveeta sneered. 'Who is?'

'But there's more!' Allura exclaimed. 'I asked about the gods. Did the kings and queens not bow to them? He lifted me in his arms and asked if I could see him. Of course, I told him, what a silly question. He then asked if I thought he was strong and did I feel protected in his arms? Again I said yes. Satisfied, he carried me to the altar in the very chapel we were yesterday. "Here," he turned me slowly in a circle so I could see the relics, "are your gods and goddesses. Would you like them to hold you, to care for you as I do?"

'"But these are statues," I said, "and pictures." He nodded, pleased with my answer.

'"And so would any wise person say," he added. "A king is here and now and made of flesh and blood, a god is a story, a legend represented by objects."'

'I have faith,' said Saraveeta, 'as must all who are oppressed. Without our unseen gods to appeal to, we would have nothing but the all too visible tyrants of this world.'

'I do not wish to be a tyrant, Saraveeta.'

'You are in no danger of that,' Saraveeta assured her. 'If anything, you are more likely to lose your freedom altogether.'

'To the baron?' Saraveeta allowed her to answer the question herself. 'But he has taken me as his wife, not his slave.'

'The baron has taken you, that's it,' Saraveeta corrected. 'Haven't you seen that?'

'I will fight him. We will both fight him. You will help me.'

'I take no orders from you anymore.'

'Then do it as a friend.'

'Let's concentrate on the moment, princess. I want you to come for me, now.'

Allura's body began to spasm, the words having their own secret enveloping power. 'Yes,' she hissed. 'Oh, yes…' and so she orgasmed, the dildo inside her, the future vastly uncertain, both in terms of her own fate and that of the kingdom.

I shall pray, she thought to herself. I shall rediscover these deities I have neglected so long on my father's advice. And maybe I will recover something of my honor, and my family's honor.

Chapter Seven

For the next five days the princess was not permitted to leave the baron's quarters. Nor was she permitted the dignity of clothing. When she wanted a drink it was from the bowl on the floor, and when she wanted to eat it was from the food bowl beside it. The baron did not return for her in all this time, nor did Saraveeta, and Allura imagined them together, enjoying each other and cohabitating like the traitorous vermin they were.

Allura was afraid that the servants would learn of her humiliating predicament, but interestingly enough the baron sent only his soldiers to bring her food and water. These men were largely indifferent to her naked charms, and if they wanted her they gave no indication. More than likely they were under orders not to touch her, but she did not care for them having the right to look at her, and covered herself with a blanket when any of them appeared.

Except for Tesotoro. She told herself she would use the man to her own ends, but there was little reason to suppose he would be on her side more than any of the others. She was not sure what it was about him that was different; perhaps the fact that his hair was blond like hers – a great rarity in the kingdom. Or maybe it was the gentleness of his hands as he had bound her – gentle, yet very, very arousing. He'd had her excited without any actual sexual advance.

When it was his shift to bring water and food she would take it, crawling to his feet. The others be damned; she would throw the bowls in their faces. Word got round and Tesotoro took ribbing about his little pet.

'What's your secret, Tesotoro, did you give her a little barbarian injection to tame her?' she would hear them taunting. So he was a barbarian; that would explain the blond hair, though it did not explain how he'd come into the service of a noble of her civilized country. She would find this out, one way or another.

Apparently word got back to the baron about Tesotoro, and finally he came to her, exceedingly angry. 'Did you spread it for him?' he demanded, grabbing her by the back of her neck.

'No,' she wailed, 'I swear it.'

He cuffed her. 'You're a lying cunt,' he spat. 'The rumors fly all over the castle. You sniff after him like a bitch in heat.'

'It is nothing,' she promised, tears in her eyes. 'Nothing at all.'

He stared at her, scowling. 'I will punish you for this. Regardless of what you did or did not do, an example must be set.'

'But that isn't fair,' she protested, employing the phrase she so often found herself using to such little effect as of late.

He pushed her to her knees and thrust his cock between her lips. 'I won't be made a fool of, Allura,' he vowed, the princess sucking obediently, grateful for the chance to appease him. 'This will cost you dungeon time,' he informed her gruffly. 'Three days.'

Allura sucked more eagerly in an effort to change his mind, but as he ejaculated in the back of her throat, compelling her to swallow his copious issue, he remained steadfast. 'It won't be pleasant but you'll survive it, just like Saraveeta.'

'Is that what this is,' she asked when she'd swallowed his seed, 'a shoddy way to win revenge on behalf of your new slut? Maybe you should have married her and not me.'

The baron frowned, but instead of being angry he seemed amused. 'Do I detect a note of jealousy?'

'You detect contempt, Montreico, which is all you deserve.'

The baron tucked away his deflated penis. 'Rodolfo will escort you to your new quarters, my dear,' he said mildly. 'Do give my regards to the rats and the spiders.'

'I hate you with all my heart!' she cried. 'I despise you more than you will ever know!'

'Oh well,' he shrugged, 'I suppose I'll have to live with that, won't I?'

He left her alone to wait for Rodolfo, the man looking stiff and somber as he came to fetch her. 'I'll have to shackle you.' He held out the heavy chain, clutched in his fists.

'Rodolfo, take pity on me,' she pleaded, lowering her face to his feet, her golden hair draped over his boots.

'Princess, do not make a spectacle of yourself.'

'But this is only between us.' She looked up at him. 'I know what you feel for me. I can see it in your eyes. Why should we not share a life together?'

'Give me your wrists,' he ordered.

She held them up. 'Rodolfo, I do have feelings for you.'

'As you do for Tesotoro and whoever else happens to be holding your leash at the time.'

Allura blushed. He was accusing her of being a slut or a treacherous user or men. She wished she understood how it all worked; both were true, and neither were. 'But Rodolfo,' she decided to appeal to his ambition, 'do you not see the opportunities for a man like you? I've watched you. I know you chafe under the baron's yoke. I can give you power beyond your wildest dreams.'

The shackles closed tightly and heavily on her wrists. 'You will be quiet,' the man instructed, 'or face the consequences.'

'You mean there is something worse than the dungeon?' She laughed darkly. 'I find that hard to believe.'

'Arms in the air,' he commanded. 'On your feet.' Allura stood, holding aloft her chained wrists. 'There is always something worse.' He produced an iron collar with a heavy padlock, and it weighed low on Allura's shoulders as he snapped it shut.

'I'm afraid,' she whispered timorously as the metal locked.

'Put your hands behind my head,' Rodolfo commanded, ignoring her words, then he abruptly pulled her tight against him and kissed her, his tongue invading her mouth, and she had no choice but to stand there and let him have his way.

By the time he released her she was panting. 'Rodolfo, don't stop...' she pleaded in hushed, breathless tones.

'I cannot go on like this,' he stated, his voice a low growl. 'The temptation overwhelms me. That is why I must put this on you without delay.' Allura beheld the iron belt, designed to fit about her naked middle, sealing off her sexual parts to any not privileged with the key. 'By order of the baron you will wear this until freed from the dungeon. None will remove it but he, none will have you till he commands it.'

She swallowed nervously. 'But what if I have to pee?' she asked, the first foolish question that came to mind.

'There is a grate in the front,' he informed her. 'You will urinate through it. This is for your own good, princess. You would be mightily abused in the dungeon without it.'

'But... but won't I still be vulnerable?'

'Your ass and your mouth will not be guarded,' he confirmed, and only now did the full implications of her sentence begin to sink in. Maybe she wouldn't survive. Maybe she wasn't strong enough to.

'Rodolfo, please make love to me first,' she begged shamelessly. 'Let me go down there with the memory of your cock inside me.'

'The belt,' he said dismissively, 'I must put it on. The baron holds the only key.'

'Don't lock me away,' she rubbed her front against him, 'not yet.' She told herself it was all part of her stratagem, to keep herself free as long as possible, but there were needs in her soul, shameless needs, and if the baron could or would not fill them then she must look elsewhere.

'Bitch!' He pushed her, flinging her to the floor. 'Why do you torment me?'

Allura had no shame. She was desperate. 'Fuck me,' she begged, but Rodolfo shook with rage, fists clenched. Never had she seen a man so divided against himself; a man so determined to fight his own desires. 'Please,' she instinctively sought and found the key word, *'master.'* And she succeeded, the baron's right-hand man falling on her as if indeed she were a slave.

'I'll fuck you straight to hell,' he cursed, and she fought for air as the man's erection impaled her smoothly and fully. She felt so small beneath him, so vulnerable.

Over and over he told her what a treacherous bitch she was, but he never once slowed his assault, Allura pounded into submission. She may have begged for it, but now it was being imposed and she tipped into the orgasm she craved. If only she could see tomorrow. If only she could feel again some sense of control over her own destiny.

'Clean yourself,' he commanded, rising from her and finding a rag. 'Time is wasting.' As best she could with shackled wrists and no water she wiped away the evidence of their union from between her thighs. 'Legs apart,' he ordered as he tugged her arms above her head again, and the belt creaked as he put it on her. It was snugger than she'd hoped, and in one way it gave her a feeling of safety and protection, but when the mechanism locked she shuddered with dread.

'We have to do the ankles too,' he said, kneeling at her feet, and Allura saw the ankle shackles had some chain between them, enough for her to shuffle along but no more.

'Rodolfo,' she asked softly, 'will you come and visit me?'

'I have many duties, princess. I can make no promises.' His answer, cold and dispassionate, frightened her. Was he writing her off as too much trouble to be bothered with?

'I wish to see Saraveeta,' she said, 'before I am taken below.'

'That is not authorized, princess.'

'Then make it so, unless you would like me to share with the baron what has just occurred between us.'

He cocked his head warily. 'Blackmail?' he mused. 'I warn you, you are on unsafe ground.'

'Rodolfo,' she persisted, 'grant my request and I shall drop the matter forever.'

He pursed his lips, thoughtful. 'I shall take you at your word,' he decided.

'Thank you.' He would never be more than a fool, she thought, the kind of man who would turn down the world on a platter for some intangible sense of honor.

Saraveeta came to her wearing a dress of red and a gold wrap around her shoulder and below one arm.

'You look more and more like slave royalty every day,' said Allura.

The girl touched her new collar, solid gold, a little defensively. 'The baron is pleased to treat me this way. I have no say in the matter.'

'Even when it comes to punishing me?'

'I took my revenge already,' said a much more subdued Saraveeta. 'I bear you no more ill will. You may consider yourself forgiven.'

Allura was instantly suspicious. 'What's come over you?' she demanded. 'Is something going on between you and the baron?'

The girl remained expressionless, neither warm nor cold. 'It's nothing I could explain to someone like you, no offense. You called for me, Allura. I assume you have some purpose in mind?'

'Do you mean am I going to plead for you to intervene with your new friend, or whatever he is, to keep me from the dungeon? No, anything but.' Actually that was precisely her plan, but seeing the renewed fortunes of her old friend only made her the more determined to endure her own sufferings with pride. 'I was simply going to ask you to get word to my uncle that I am doing well.'

'And are you doing well, Allura?'

She held up her chains, jangling them. 'Never better. This iron jewelry is ever so much more practical than gold, don't you think?'

'I think,' Saraveeta replied grimly, 'that you have been through too much since your arrival and that the baron has no business putting you in the dungeon.'

Now it was Allura's turn to be surprised. 'You would defend me after I had you thrown in a dungeon?'

'We must all grow as people, Allura. If we keep on passing the same bad experiences back and forth we will never overcome hate.' Saraveeta pulled a tiny vial from the folds of her dress. 'This is a drug, Allura, it will dull the pain for a while and make the transition easier.'

The princess allowed Saraveeta to put it to her lips, and almost immediately she felt the effects. The room seemed more distant, her heart laboring in her chest.

'Saraveeta...' Allura slurred the name of her friend, 'will you hug me now... and let me tell you... I'm sorry?' Allura felt her consciousness slipping away; she heard voices, Saraveeta's reassuring touch, saw faces blurred and colorful.

Two of the baron's men carried her, one holding her legs, the other underneath her arms. She wondered if she was heavy for them with all her chains. Would they ache in the morning from the strain or did they do this sort of thing all the time? Strange the things that go through a person's head in such bizarre circumstances.

'It's cold,' Allura complained as they wound down the ancient, spiral stone steps to the threatening world below. 'I'll catch my death down here.'

The guards chuckled. 'Ain't much by the way of fancy fireplaces down here,' said one, tall and thin like a reed.

'Or good candlelight, neither,' added the second, who seemed as squat as a teakettle with copper teeth.

Their shadows grew longer and more jagged, and at the bottom level the teakettle thrust her into the arms of the reed and took a burning torch from a bracket on the wall. 'Hey, she's too heavy for me alone,' the reed complained.

Allura giggled, thinking it was funny to see them argue, because to her they looked like characters from some silly fairytale.

'Let's just get the shackles off and put her on all fours. She needs to get used to it.'

'Good thinking.' The reed opened the various locks, removed the iron bonds and began kicking her behind. 'Get along, little doggie.'

The stone floor was damp and slimy, her palms slipped and she slumped on her front. 'Whoops,' she mumbled, wondering why her arms and legs wouldn't work.

'Hey, that's the princess,' the teakettle whistled with some alarm. 'You want to get us impaled?'

'She ain't no princess down here.' The reed kicked at her. 'She's dungeon meat like the rest. Anyway, what you think the baron sent her down here for?'

'Good point,' the kettle acknowledged. 'The only thing I don't get is why they sent her down drunk.'

'They're royalty. How should we know why they do what they do?'

'Spoken like a true philosopher.'

Now they were both shoving their boots into her ribcage, trying to get her up to her knees. She itched beneath the iron belt, feeling the pressure of their feet.

'Come on, dungeon trash,' said the kettle.

'Move it, slut,' echoed the reed, and Allura did her best, although it finally took one of the men holding her hair like a leash to keep her straight. They continued down a long dank corridor to a heavy wooden door at the end. The stench was overpowering now and Allura nearly wretched. She could feel the drug wearing off already, and by the time the door was opened her senses were once again acute.

Inside the vaulted, stone-walled chamber she saw various tortured prisoners, all female. One, in a torn peasant dress, hung on an X-shaped cross, her ankles and wrists tightly bound. Both breasts were bared and welted with the marks of a heavy whip. Her eyes followed the newcomers but she appeared too terrified to speak.

In another corner a small woman crouched naked in a cage. She was clutching a crust of bread, green with mold, tearing off occasional crumbs with her teeth. Her short black hair was matted, and a heavy iron collar was around her throat, attached to a chain that was fixed to the wall outside the cage. She crouched on straw that stank of urine.

Another woman was bound over a barrel, her buttocks red and twitching, as if from a recent beating. She was quite large, with a head of red curls that lay disheveled in the soiled straw upon the stone floor of the cell.

'What's this then?' the grizzly, bearded dungeon keeper asked as the soldiers presented the naked blonde. The shabbily dressed, claw-fingered hunchback of a man barely looked up from his work, which involved clamping nasty iron jaws onto the breasts of a naked, gagged girl. She looked to be eighteen or so, and was tied down on a wooden table.

'No less a person than the baron's new wife,' said the reed, who no longer looked quite so bizarre, now that the drug had worn off. 'And the crown princess to boot.'

'Boil my balls in oil,' the dungeon keeper grumbled. 'Can't that whelp handle his own woman problems? Can't he see I'm up to my eyeballs down here?'

'Apparently she's tougher than she looks,' said the teakettle, who now resembled nothing more than a squat guard with an overbite.

'Is that right?' the keeper asked Allura directly, the fingers of one hand deep in the pussy of the suffering girl, making her moan amidst her tears. 'You a difficult little cunt to manage? Reckon so,' he answered himself. 'Never met a highborn bitch that wasn't. So what's she down for, the works?'

'Everything but the pussy,' the reed confirmed. 'And you've got three days to do it in.'

'No pussy, you say?' the keeper grumbled. 'So how am I supposed to do my job if I can't get in her workings good and proper?'

'Ass and mouth are open.'

'I should hope so,' the keeper snorted. 'Can't tell me to break a bitch and not have those to work with.'

'Where you want her, then?'

'String her up over yonder. And crank those chains for me while you're at it. Get her swinging for me, if you don't mind.'

The two guards dragged Allura to a set of chains hanging from the ceiling at eye level. Clasping one shut on each wrist, they worked the crank on the wall gradually lifting her to tiptoes and finally off her feet entirely.

'A lovely sight.' The teakettle gave her a push, letting her swing.

'Anything else?' asked the reed, sounding a little anxious to get out of the ominous place and back to the light of day and fresh air.

'We'll leave you to it then,' said the kettle, looking equally keen to get out of the dungeon.

'No…' Allura cried, but to no avail as the two guards, tall and short, slammed the heavy wooden door behind them.

'Hush,' the keeper ordered, 'or I'll gag you.'

'Please, master,' gasped the pale young woman with the iron jaws on her breasts, 'I'll tell you all you want to know. I had three accomplices. One worked at the inn and the other two—'

The man brutally shoved a gag in her mouth. 'Demon's balls,' he grumbled, 'now I remember why I shut you up before. You talk too much.'

She shook her head, sobbing; begging frantically with her eyes, but the loathsome man had eyes only for her pain, and the way it made her youthful body contort and writhe.

'Confound my desiccated old cock,' he grumbled, and Allura watched him masturbate, his eyes bulging and his jaw tightening, using the suffering of the girl on the table as an aphrodisiac.

'You, royal cunt,' he growled at Allura, 'tell me something to make me harder.' She stared, openmouthed. 'Do it,' he threatened, 'or I'll bite these little beauties clean off.' He had his gnarled fingers on the screws of the jaws.

'But what shall I tell you?' she cried. 'I have no idea what you want to hear.'

'Tell me what you're willing to do to keep me from skewering your nipples with needles.'

Allura hung helplessly, clenching and unclenching her fists. 'You cannot do that to me,' she challenged. 'Don't you know who I am?'

'Sure I do,' he said glibly. 'You're a three-day fix it job. No access to the cunt. Lydia, any reason I can't skewer nipples on a three day job?'

The woman on the cross, with the whipped breasts, gazed with blank eyes. 'No, master.'

The man chuckled gleefully as he pulled out a long set of tongs. 'I'm waiting, princess. Time to talk and save your little sister here.' He lifted the device over the pussy of the tortured girl, one handle in each of his craggy hands.

'I-I would do anything you said,' Allura blurted. 'Anything at all.'

'Too vague.' He squeezed the pincers shut on the tiny pink nub between the girl's thighs, making her jerk against her bonds. 'Isn't she a work of art?' he sighed. 'The way her body responds to pain is quite something.' He moved the pincers from place to place, over her labia and back to her clitoris, and with fine manipulations he won from her an emphatic spasm.

'I would give you pleasure,' offered the princess, presenting the first thing that came to her mind to divert the man. 'Wouldn't you like that?'

'Be still my beating heart.' The sarcasm was not lost, nor was the sudden arching of the girl's back and the way she turned to Allura with pleading eyes.

'Wait, I'll do more,' Allura blurted. 'I'll do anything you want me too.'

The loathsome brute seemed intrigued by this offer, dropped the tongs and shuffled over to her.

'What's the matter,' he croaked as she cringed away from him, his bloodshot eyes boring into her, his breath fetid, 'can't handle a real man?'

'Please, just let me go,' she begged. 'I can get you anything you want.'

'Why would I want anything?' he scoffed. 'I'm living and working in paradise.' The dungeon keeper pinched her nipples, alternating pain with an odd, shameful pleasure.

'D-don't touch me,' she groaned.

'Oh, giving orders, are we?' He smacked her face, leaving an instant, blotchy handprint on her cheek. 'You're forgetting, I give the orders down here. Apologize to me, your better.'

'I'm... sorry,' she whispered.

'Sorry, master,' he corrected. 'Down here I'm your master.'

'Yes, I'm sorry master.'

'I'm the lord of this particular manor, and you're nothing more than a slut, the lowliest of bitches.'

'Yes, master, I'm a slut and a lowly bitch.'

He smacked her other cheek. 'Not lowly; lowliest.'

'Sorry,' she corrected pitifully. 'Please don't be angry with me.'

'Oh, I don't want to be angry,' he mocked. 'I lose sleep worrying that I might be too angry with you dears, but what can we do?' He scratched his stubbly jaw exaggeratedly, as though trying to solve a problematic puzzle. 'Aha, I know…'

The dungeon keeper limped away to a dingy corner, rummaged around for a few moments, and then returned with a fearsome, coiled whip, and Allura shivered at the ominous presence of it.

'This whip is made for use on animals,' he informed her, somewhat unnecessarily. 'Are you an animal, slut?'

Allura feared a trick question. 'I-I don't know, master.'

'Then I shall have to educate you, shall I not?' he drawled, brushing the leather coils over her treacherously hard nipples. 'A whip like this doesn't just punish a female,' he went on, Allura barely hearing his goading ramblings, 'it fucks her.'

Allura accepted the handle pressed to her lips, and without being told she parted them and he pushed it deep, her jaw aching as her mouth filled with pungent leather. Frightening herself with her obedience she sucked, wanting the feel of it all the way to the back of her throat, the smell and taste of leather filling her nostrils and her mouth, mingling sickeningly with the dungeon keeper's odor and the stench of the foreboding dungeon, and the constant pull of the cuffs on her wrists, pulling her body so vulnerably taut as she hung there.

'How about it?' He removed the saliva coated handle from between her lips. 'Ready to be whipped?'

She had no way to resist; no reserves of strength, no

option left except to accept. 'Y-yes, master,' she whispered meekly, and he cackled smugly, shuffling behind her. She was braced but not truly ready, knowing something terrible was coming, but unprepared for quite how terrible.

At first he merely ran the coils up and down her back, and expecting so much worse she was caught off guard, frightened of being lured into a false sense of security.

'You've a fine backside,' he praised lewdly. 'That's how a young filly ought to be, with an ass ripe for whipping.'

The odious wretch pulled back his wiry arm, and Allura heard the whip dragging back on the dirty stone floor and grimly braced herself.

Her screams filled the small chamber as the lash bit into her back and she twisted and writhed in her bonds.

The scrawny arm reared back again and delivered another cruel lash, cutting through her senses, sending her emotions soaring.

'How many,' he taunted. 'How many marks for the lady today? Ten, my fair slut, or did I hear twenty?'

'None, master, please…'

'Nine?' he teased. 'Did you say nine?'

Three times more, in a lattice style across her back and buttocks, he worked his hellish strokes, welts in red and blue, the colors of torture, working the froth of sadistic ecstasy.

'And they say a humble servant such as myself can't enjoy his work,' he mused, the sole audience for his own distorted humor. 'Ah, for a mirror,' he sighed admiring his handiwork.

'Am I well marked, dungeon keeper?' Allura whispered. 'I trust you did your work well?'

'I know my art,' he said.

'You must describe it to me. I want to know as well as feel… please, do not keep me waiting.'

'Fine lines, well placed,' he told her. 'A slut's marking, crisscrossing your back.'

'Are there bruises,' she pressed, 'and welts? I have to know it all.'

'They are a thing of beauty,' he confirmed, 'and will leave you marked a fair long while.'

'And any who sees me,' she followed the dark reasoning, 'will know what happened to me. They'll know I was here, a punished dungeon slut. What an irony this is. Do you know how many I have sent to dungeons like this? Do you think we are any different, you and me?'

'I'd say being on one side of the whip or the other makes plenty of difference.'

'My slaves lived in terror of me,' she reflected, lost in her reverie. 'They knew from the time I was a little girl that there was a coldness in my eyes.'

'Indicating what?' He was licking the sweat from her back, but she barely seemed to notice his lurid attention.

'Indicating my penchant for preying on the weak.'

'Ah,' he chuckled, 'as I do.'

'Punish me for it,' she pleaded.

'Are you daring me or mocking me?' The dungeon keeper released her from her bonds. 'Whichever, you are madder than I,' he concluded, dragging her across the floor, 'so some time in the hold is what you need to regain your senses.'

The hold lay behind a heavy door of iron through which shone no light. There were no windows, no openings of any kind.

'Have fun, my sweet,' said the dungeon keeper, slamming shut the foreboding door, locking her inside, condemned to solitary darkness, and there she was left to dwell on the defeat of the baron, how she would survive this hell and emerge, stronger, his worst nightmare.

Chapter Eight

Allura spoke to no one of her time in the dungeon. The last thing she did before her release was to look the dungeon keeper in the eye and spit upon him, but it seemed a strangely endearing gesture, done with an oddly chilling smile that he seemed to appreciate.

'Until we meet again,' he drawled, wiping the insult from his face, touching it to his thin, colorless lips.

'That will not be upon this earth,' she replied.

'In hell, then,' he chuckled.

The dress the baron provided for Allura was of yellow silk, trimmed in white lace. It was a perfect fit, hugging her trim waist and shapely bosom, exposing her tantalizing, shadowy cleavage. She would drive the hateful man mad with desire, the prospect of which delightedly her greatly, for she was determined that he would never receive pleasure from her again.

Rodolfo arrived to escort her down to the great hall, and the look of chagrin on his face was all the encouragement she needed to damn him to his face. 'I am surprised you have the audacity to continue breathing the air of this world, Rodolfo, being a man of no honor,' she said. 'Are you so afraid of death as to deny the mercy that might come from the gods as a result of a cleansing suicide?'

He attempted to hide his deep disgrace. 'I seek to follow my orders, that is my place in life.'

'Orders?' she scoffed. 'And from whom do you take them? Your evil baron or the demon seed that rules your heart?'

He took her arm, leading her downstairs. 'Once you spoke to me of a common alliance, princess,' he said conspiratorially. 'I would talk of it again. The truth is I think of you every night. I dream of you.'

'Do you love me?'

'I do, yes.'

'Very well, await my orders,' she told him, smiling triumphantly within as he left her at the entrance to the great hall.

Allura held her head high as she walked across the marble floor. It had been an emotional day, a topsy-turvy day; from the depths of despair she'd been restored to her former status, at least by virtue of clothing. But where did she stand? Who was the baron to her? Did he love her, hate her, or both? Would he punish her? One battle upon another, the man seeming to back down only to attack again with even more vigor.

And now he was sitting upon his high chair, looking every bit as arrogant as the day she'd first seen him lounging on her father's throne. She could not help but think of herself upon the floor, groveling for the apple peel with her lips.

'Wife, come and sit beside me,' he called, beckoning languidly with one hand, and she did so, perching uncomfortably on the seat beside his.

'You look lovely, my dear,' he drooled, kissing her hand, but she said nothing as she surveyed the finely dressed people gathered in the hall, men and women from the highest born houses.

'What is the purpose of all this, Montreico?' she eventually asked.

'Tonight you become queen,' he informed her. 'It is your uncle we await. He has agreed to give us his blessing, and the nobles in turn will clear the way to granting you queen.'

'With you naturally positioned as the power behind the throne,' she added dryly

'Cynicism does not suit you,' he sniggered.

'Evil plotting, however, seems to suit you just fine,' she countered, becoming more focused by the minute, the greed and malevolence of the man so obvious. But soon these traits would be his own downfall.

At that moment there was a commotion, some guards opening the great doors and entering the hall, their spears aggressively ready. A single courtier was ushered in, the man dressed in purple with a feathered cap. He stopped midway between the dais and the door and cleared his throat with ceremonial, if not theatrical aplomb.

'The Grand Duke Fortragian,' he announced, and the grand duke, who seemed rather annoyed by the fuss, strode directly past him. The baron stood and stepped down, preparing to greet him at the end of the red carpet. Allura remained seated, by virtue of her office.

'Fortragian,' the baron followed his bow with a hearty clasp of the older man's hand, 'you do us a great honor.'

'You gave me little choice, Montreico,' he grumbled. 'Really, a man of my age and position should hardly be summoned on a moment's notice. What could possibly be so urgent? And furthermore, what of these rumors at court concerning your treatment of the princess, and your lack of piety to the gods? If this is some attempt to legitimate a false position on your part—'

'Not at all.' The baron looked calm enough, but Allura was sure he was bluffing. If there were some groundswell against him it would only be a matter of time before the peers acted, or the body of high priests.

Yet the dukes and barons were assembled, and many of the high priests as well, so what trick did Montreico have up his sleeve?

'In fact, Fortragian, I am prepared to not only defend my position but to raise it to one of complete and sacred unassailability,' the baron said confidently. 'And to this end I offer a witness; one whose word exceeds that of all the priests, whose legitimacy surpasses that of all the nobles put together. Need I spell it out any further?'

'I have no taste for guessing games, Montreico,' said the old man harshly. 'Produce your evidence and your witness now or I shall take my leave, having considered this journey a waste of time.'

'Very well, I shall,' the baron continued smoothly. 'Ladies and gentlemen, I present to you the Intentionary Priestess, the Sublime Ekalianuma, Tertia the Fifteenth.'

A collective gasp was drawn from those assembled.

'Montreico, what are you babbling about?' demanded the grand duke.

'It is true, she is here and she will auger on my behalf.'

'No intentionary priestess has left the Ekalia Temple for centuries, baron. What you speak is impossible.'

'All things are possible, grand duke,' spoke a conceitedly melodic voice. 'It is merely that we do not know the ingredients to call them into being.'

'Mother Seer,' croaked the old man, who had just seen something to widen even his jaded old eyes.

'Be at ease,' she touched his elbow. 'All shall be well.'

Allura wondered what that meant, or indeed why a figure of such utter recluse and sacred value in their land would come to the castle of a mere baron and for such a completely non-religious purpose.

'The Great Mother Seer has come to testify and give

her blessing to this ascension to the throne of Princess Allura, with myself as husband, as well as protector and guardian of the realm,' the baron announced.

So that was it. He planned to name himself de facto king. But surely the priestess would not support such a thing.

'I shall speak what I have come to speak,' the holy woman confirmed. 'No more, no less.'

'May I ask, great lady, that you turn to face the assembly?' The baron could hardly control the gloating in his voice. 'I believe they all need to hear this.' The odious man was about to get everything he wanted, and without drawing a drop of blood in conflict.

The priestess, whose hooded white robe covered her slender frame entirely from neck to toe, turned and lifted her arms to the stunned assembly. Not one dared speak a word; few scarcely could believe the evidence of their own senses. It was indeed an event, a presence most unprecedented.

'People before me, and those not before me, to all who hear these words spoken and those who do not, to those above and below, fore and aft the grave, hear this auger,' the woman declared in the obfuscating terms of a religious leader. 'A warning do I give unto this house and to this land. A curse do I expose.'

Now it was the baron's turn for a shock. 'Priestess, what is this you are saying?' he demanded. 'This is not as we discussed!'

It was Rodolfo who restrained him as he attempted to seize her. 'Sir, have you lost your mind?' he warned. 'It is damnation to lay hands upon the priestess!'

'Let the priestess speak,' commanded the grand duke. 'We shall be to the bottom of this outrage at last.'

'She,' the priestess wheeled about to face the seated

Allura, 'is not the true issue of the king. She is abomination and she must never sit upon the throne.'

At once swords were drawn, by the grand duke's men and by the baron's alike. Cries could be heard throughout the hall and sounds of protest. Allura herself put a hand to her breast as though stabbed. It was not possible. The priestess was speaking a lie, a most vile and destructive falsehood.

'Silence!' commanded Fortragian, recovering for the moment the mettle of his youth. 'Any who disrupts this assembly shall perish by my own hand! Holy priestess, we humbly bid you, explain yourself.'

'She is not the daughter of the former king,' the priestess repeated. 'A second time I say this, and now a third. She is imposter set in place of the true heir. Place her over your lands as queen, place upon her head the crown and you shall be cursed unto the end of time.'

'But this cannot be!' the baron cried. 'Priestess, you already said to me it would be an issue of this house – my house – that would one day be king, the legitimate and rightful ruler! How can this be if I have married an imposter? Are you saying now I have bedded this whore Allura for nothing? You have deceived me!'

Fortragian's dagger pressed to the baron's throat. 'Speak one more word concerning my niece, Montreico, and I swear I'll slay you or die in the effort.'

The baron made no effort to disarm the elderly duke. His eyes were on the woman in the white robe and his fists were clenched. 'Speak,' he said to the priestess, his voice taking upon itself a tone Allura knew well and feared. It was the same tone that preceded her own worst punishments at his hands. 'Make this right, great lady, while it is still possible.'

'All I have said then and now is consistent,' said the

priestess, unperturbed. 'An issue of this house shall be king. But you shall not be its father, nor she its mother.'

'But I am baron,' he snarled, pointing to the shields upon the wall. 'My crest. My castle. My authority.'

'This one,' the priestess pointed to the shocked Rodolfo, 'shall succeed you as baron. And he shall wed the true princess.'

'What true princess?' Fortragian cried. 'I understand nothing of what you speak.'

'Behold the rightful issue; the blood royale.' The priestess raised a finger, sacred and fortuitous, and all waited with bated breath as her eyes scanned the room and she pointed, finally, to a humble slave kneeling at the side of the court, in a row of others, the property of the baron. 'Her. She is the true daughter of the king.'

It was Allura who reacted first. 'Saraveeta!' she cried. 'But how?'

'The king long ago reversed your identities,' the priestess began to explain, 'upon your birth, Allura, just three months behind that of your dearest friend. Under pain of death he compelled Saraveeta's family to accept his own daughter while he took you to be his.'

'You are mad,' Allura hissed. 'My father would never do such a thing!'

'The king was many things, but not mad. He followed the will of she who preceded me. The former priestess knew a usurper would come, one who would wed the royal heir and seek to claim the throne falsely for himself... and that man is him.'

Now it was the baron being pointed out.

'This is babble,' he declared furiously. 'This woman is the princess, and she is my wife.'

'Let go of me,' cried Allura as Montreico seized her arm.

'The king knew there was only one way to save his daughter and to save the kingdom,' the priestess continued calmly, as if nothing were occurring around her. 'And that way was to raise his daughter in obscurity.'

The bite of Montreico's grip brought Allura's thoughts into focus. This logic was exactly the sort her father – if he was still her father – would use. And wouldn't this fit with what he had always told her about not loving anyone when a sovereign? But why then had he told her that she was part of him, and how could he have behaved as he did, showering love and affection on her all those years to the exclusion of his real progeny? One thing this did explain, though, was why Saraveeta always beat her in everything in their youth.

'Lies!' Montreico bellowed. 'Lies! Lies!'

'We shall enquire further,' said the grand duke. 'Bring both Allura and Saraveeta to a private chamber and we'll examine them both.'

Montreico bundled aside Allura and leapt for Saraveeta. 'There will be no enquiries,' he growled, seizing her from behind, holding his blade to the slave's throat. 'Henceforth you all take my orders.'

'Baron, what brand of insanity is this?' demanded Fortragian.

'Call it an insurance policy. Rodolfo, fetch me the other slut as well.'

Rodolfo, looking more than a little uncomfortable, but obeying nonetheless, snatched Allura's wrist and manhandled her to the baron, where drawing his sword, Montreico pointed it at the blonde girl's throat. 'There, now I am covered both ways. Disobey me and I kill both.'

'The gods curse you for this, Montreico!' Fortragian barked.

'Silence, old man,' he snarled back. 'Rodolfo, clap him

in irons.'

The grand duke's guards gathered around him protectively, ready to lay down their lives.

'Best have them drop their weapons,' warned the baron. 'They are outnumbered and you of all people should know I am not bluffing.'

'Do it,' ordered the grand duke to his men. 'Lay down your weapons.'

'Now take them all,' commanded the baron, once the arms were discarded on the floor. 'Put them in the dungeon, except for the old fool. He'll stay and watch. And seal the hall; no one escapes. Secure the carriages and horses of all assembled.'

The hall was quickly ringed with troops, and more were pouring in through the doors, and like a noose about their collective necks, swords and spears encircled the lords and ladies.

'I shall have all weapons,' he called out. 'You are all my guests as before, only now you shall obey me as king. For that is what I am, as soon as this bitch of a priestess recants. Rodolfo, put these sluts upon the dais, tie them to the chairs, and give me archers. I want archers at every corner of this hall. Anyone who disrupts the proceedings here is to be eliminated at once.'

'Montreico, you can't do this,' said Allura, the man's chest against her back, but Saraveeta took her hand, clenching it tightly.

'Let it be,' she whispered. 'All will be well.'

Allura turned to her, the young woman so calm. Did she know she was the true princess? Could she have known all along, at least subconsciously?

'Shut up both of you,' Montreico growled. 'Don't give me an excuse to cut out both your tongues.'

'You're a dead man,' Saraveeta vowed at Montreico,

as Rodolfo led them to the chairs. 'There will be no escape for you.'

The baron nearly ran her through there and then, but held himself back, and raising his sword instead he addressed the assembly. 'Ladies and gentlemen, you are truly fortunate tonight, for not only will you witness a coronation, you will also behold an augury taken under torture in order that we might expose the lies of this so-called priestess.'

'This is blasphemy!' cried Fortragian. 'No man may harm the high priestess! You will lay a curse of blackness a thousand years deep on this land.'

'If I torture a priestess, yes,' agreed the madly grinning, wild-eyed baron, 'but not if I torture a slave. Slave testimony, including auguries, must be taken under torture. This is holy law, is it not?'

'It is, but the holy priestess is not, and cannot ever be made a slave. The very idea is blasphemy.'

All eyes watched and followed as Montreico, sword and dagger still in hand, walked deliberately towards the white-robed woman, who in all the fracas had not moved an inch. Nor did she flinch as the baron ran the side of his glinting blade lightly down her robed arm. 'Right again, duke, but there is nothing that says a priestess cannot ask to be a slave. What do you think, great lady, could a female as high as you be induced to want to change her station so drastically? I know the legends, that your kind are the most beautiful of women and that you hide a passion deeper than any underground river of fire.'

The priestess said nothing.

'Montreico, you must stop,' Fortragian appealed, his voice cracking.

'Gag him,' ordered the baron. 'And put him in a chair next to the sluts. I want him to have a good view of the festivities.'

The grand duke looked more distressed than Allura had ever seen him, and she feared he would have a seizure. How cruel was the baron, insane with power and utterly without regard for human life? And it seemed he held all the cards, too, the high priestess, the duke, and the true princess – whichever of them that might be – all in his clutches.

'I'll protect you,' whispered Rodolfo as he tied the old man next to her.

'You've done a great job so far,' Allura could not help but observe.

'Priestess,' Montreico declared for the benefit of all, 'before we begin I give you this opportunity to spare yourself. Declare yourself my slave now, openly, and I promise you will not face the tortures I have planned.' The baron was met with stubborn silence. 'Again,' he said, 'I ask you to capitulate. Priestess though you may be, you are a woman and your body will betray you. You bring this upon yourself,' he warned, but the priestess remained as she was. 'Very well, this is on your head.'

Dropping his weapons to the floor he seized the hood of her robe, and tugging it down he tore at her clothes, the assault combining with a crack of lightning that filled the hall. Allura could feel the tearing inside her, and then there was an ominous, deafening rumble of thunder, the very hall seeming to shake with its ferocity. Allura clutched the arms of the chair for fear of being shaken from it, staring at the light pouring from within the shredded robe of the priestess, as if the baron had torn open a sack of iridescent grain, or unleashed a whelming flood of moon water. People were screaming, falling to the floor. She turned her head from the overabundance of the terrible light and it was then she saw Saraveeta gazing at it, with that combination of infinite fascination and holy knowing belonging to a small child.

Who was Saraveeta, or what was she? Even a princess, if that's what she was, ought to be shocked by what was happening.

'By the arms of Zuranos,' shouted a man, beholding the glaring light, 'it's an apparition!'

'The angel of death!' cried a woman.

'We're doomed,' moaned another, as Allura looked back to the priestess. The robe was liquid on the floor and something stood there – something shimmering. She thought she saw a snake and then a terrible black skeleton covered in dust. She felt the ash of it on her tongue; it was so real. But then in the blink of an eye it all changed again.

'There, you see!' called the baron in triumph, his underlying fear more than a little evident. 'This is what she is underneath. All else you saw was sorcerer's tricks. This is real.'

Before them stood a young woman with luxuriant red hair and the body of a goddess. She was splendidly naked, a jewel in her belly button. Her skin was creamy white and smooth, and begged to be touched.

'A naked female, nothing more,' said the baron. 'And we know what to do with one of them, don't we boys?'

The guards remained motionless and silent. There was not one in the chamber who did not rest uneasy with what Montreico was doing.

'What, are you still afraid?' he scoffed. 'Cowards. Behold how a real man deals with such a situation.' Retrieving his sword he passed it below her ear, lifting her lustrous red hair. 'You and I are going to be well acquainted, priestess.'

The woman looked in his eyes, the pale blue of her own

reflecting the darkness of his.

'Remove your sandals,' commanded the baron, and with great poise she obeyed. 'Now you are barefoot before me,' he observed, 'and naked. My power over you is absolute.'

'So it would seem,' said the woman, her voice soft and seductive, and Allura felt a stirring in her tummy; the woman oozed sex and the thought of this evil man dominating her was driving her wild.

'Behold,' the baron pointed out, 'she has obeyed me; she has not disputed my power.'

'But you are armed,' the priestess observed. 'Do you need a sword to dominate me?'

'Only this one,' he leered, crudely clutching his crotch.

'Am I to be fucked, then?' she asked, such a blunt word clashing with her demure beauty, and then she inclined her head elegantly to lick the flat of his sword, melting him with a smoldering stare as she caressed the blade with her tongue. For a woman utterly distant a moment before she had become surprisingly passionate, and the baron seemed uneasy by her brazenness.

'Enough of that,' he snapped. 'You will kneel before me, you treacherous bitch.'

The priestess lowered herself with flawless grace, and unbidden her face lowered to the baron's boots, where she bestowed kisses to the leather footwear.

'You were not ordered to do that,' said he peevishly.

'Force of habit,' she said, looking up, her sultry expression enough to stiffen the cock of any man. 'This is how I serve my lord.'

'What lord?' he snapped. 'You said you're a virgin.'

'Not a human lord, but my divine lord, Zuranos.'

'What are you talking about, woman?'

'The Heavenly Father Zuranos possesses me. I am

consecrated to him. He owns me and takes from me all forms of service.'

'But the gods have no bodies.'

'They can take form. Avatars, Zuranos' favorite, is that of the man-bull. In this guise I serve him often.'

The baron was frowning. 'The gods are legends,' he said. 'They are ideas, stories.' Clearly the man was banking on the idea, given his current acts of blasphemy.

'Not to his slave girls, at least; for us he is very real.'

'Stop that. I gave no such instructions.'

The priestess was kneeling, opening his breeches. 'You were correct,' she said, ignoring his objections. 'I do respond to mastery. To Zuranos I am a mere pet. I whimper at his feet and beg his favor. When he attaches his leash to my throat I am often so overcome I must seek his immediate permission so as to release the pent-up orgasm. But now I am to be yours, for you are king and more wise than any – mortal or immortal.'

Sweat was collecting on the baron's forehead, and for the first time he seemed to be realizing the trouble he had let himself in for. 'You're lying,' he snapped. 'No god has ever laid a hand on you because they don't exist. Only humans, and they are deceitful and amorous enough to fill all the storybooks and journals of the world.'

'Zuranos likes to whip my breasts with his tongue,' she presented her porcelain-white orbs, capped with cherry nipples. 'Would you like to try? His is three feet long and burns like sulfur – when he comes to me as a snake, that is. As a bull-man it takes three of my acolytes to lick his balls, and the other priestesses serve him, but I alone bear his wrath. When he appears to us, wounded in pride or smarting from some battle with his siblings, it is I who must crawl to him, naked on my belly. He will whip me to within an inch of my life and then restore me so he can begin all over.'

'Fortragian,' the baron wheeled on him, 'do you hear these words? Now who is blaspheming? This bitch speaks of abominations between her and the father of heaven.'

'It is no abomination to serve the gods; their pleasure is supreme, that of Zuranos above all others,' she declared.

'But what of Hechira, Mother of the Gods?' Asked Saraveeta, on her feet, her face lit as if she already knew the answer.

'Ah, yes,' the priestess nodded approvingly as she opened the baron's breeches and took out his stiff cock, 'good question. The wife of Zuranos, whose jealousies for her wayward husband fuel the fires of the sun itself – yes, she comes to us as well. She rips the clothes from my body as this one did and she sniffs me over. Her nostrils smell through the repairs he does upon me. Hechira knows his odor, the scent of leather and of torture.

'Whenever she catches me out as her husband's victim I am attacked all over by her. She would tear me limb from limb and has done so already more than once. I'd have stayed that way if not for Zuranos' healing interventions. Fortunately he will not let me die, not until my replacement is chosen. Till then I remain his sex toy, ever at the ready to submit.'

Saraveeta was panting. 'Can't you feel it? Can't you taste it in the air? It's like breathing pure sex!'

Allura could feel very little, but when Saraveeta pulled her to her feet and gave her a deep kiss she began to understand a little. For whatever reason this high priestess was tapping into the libido of the females in the room. Combining them, making of them an offering to the great stone idol of the temple, the erect penis of Zuranos.

Allura moaned and pushed hard against her lover. All around the hall women attacked their male escorts or any others they could find.

'Enough!' shouted the baron. 'I will tolerate no more. Rodolfo, bring those two princess whores,' he pointed at Allura and Saraveeta, 'and follow me to the dungeon. It's time we taught this little priestess here a real lesson.'

'Should we not leave them to the dungeon keeper?' asked Rodolfo, with some trepidation.

'No, you sniveling worm, we'll handle these bitches ourselves, the old-fashioned way. That is unless you're too frightened of their female witchcraft?'

'No sir,' said he, 'I have no fear.'

The baron grabbed the red locks of the priestess and hauled her to her feet. 'We shall see, Rodolfo, all too soon, who is a true man and who is not.'

Allura's sense of foreboding was acute, the threat of the dungeon filling her with dread.

The three females were roughly manhandled below and taken directly to the dungeon keeper's macabre cell, where he kept his favorite implements. The old man was absent for the moment, so the baron ordered the priestess hung immediately from the shackles in the center of the gloomy room.

A few minutes later the dungeon keeper arrived and more torches were lit. He made a thorough examination of his new resident, saying not a word to Montreico until he was done. 'Well you've let me in for it this time, haven't you?' he grumbled.

'Relax, you've nothing to fear,' Montreico drawled. 'This is just another little bitch for us to beat into submission.'

'Ever seen the likes of this before?' the wizened man croaked hoarsely, and the baron approached the body of the hanging female; that splendid pale creature with flaming red hair, a priestess who until yesterday had never been outside the temple in her entire life, but the fact that she was now suspended on tiptoes, wrists in shackles in the dungeon of a baron, seemed to mark little distress in her countenance.

Holding the torch close to her bottom, the baron examined the tiny mark between the cleft of her cheeks. Allura, who knelt nearby in the filthy straw along with Saraveeta, had a perfectly clear view. It was a circle, with three wings projecting from the center – the mark of the sky god, the father of the heavens. 'It's a tattoo, so what?' he challenged.

'No tattoo artist I know can do this.' The keeper smacked her buttocks, instantly turning the skin red, then the mark turned a bright gold, reflecting as though the woman had some light inside her shining through.

'Don't bother me with trifles,' the baron said impatiently. 'Just give me the whip.'

'Baron, you are about to whip the property of a god,' the keeper warned, but the baron snatched the long whip that Allura knew so well from the man's clawed fingers. 'She is in my dungeon, which makes her my property. And you two,' he pointed to Allura and Saraveeta, 'you are next, so take heed.'

The baron moved behind the priestess and unfurled the threatening whip. He seemed as skilled with it as the dungeon keeper, if not more so, and leaning his body into the swing the first slash landed cleanly, the flawless flesh of the priestess bruising and reddening at once, like an angry claw had torn down her back.

'Now you will tell the truth,' declared Montreico as he lashed her over and over, her ass and back and thighs. 'You are nothing, do you hear me? A whipped slave is all you are, so confess it!'

The woman's breathing had grown ragged and tight

and she rolled back her head, her expression one of concentration, and she looked at Allura as if she were going into some kind of trance.

'Confess, damn you!' he roared, but no amount of whipping seemed to matter.

'This will not work!' shouted the dungeon keeper. 'With every lash you only beg greater disaster to befall us all!'

'I will not be questioned. I will not be disobeyed.' The baron tossed the whip aside. 'I will find another way.'

Releasing the woman from her bonds he laid her on her back. 'Let's see if we can do something about this virginity, shall we?'

She had no strength to resist him, and pulling apart her legs he penetrated her brutally with one shunt of his hips. He hadn't even bothered to remove his breeches.

'She's good and wet,' he reported, 'just like any other slut. There's your horrible witch,' he mocked the others. 'I'll bet she's fucked a dozen priests and temple servants if she's fucked one. Haven't you? Go on; keep your eyes closed, little bitch. Dream of your fake Zuranos and his huge balls and three foot tongue.'

'Father of heaven,' the dungeon keeper fell to his knees, 'forgive him. He knows not what he says. He is an ignorant, dunderheaded whelp, and has been so all his life. Would that my mother and I had fed him to the wolves as the auger advised.'

'Shut up, father,' snarled the baron, 'or I shall have you impaled.'

'So you are the true baron!' Allura exclaimed to the twisted old man.

'I was, but I got tired of all the responsibility,' he answered. 'I like it much better down here. Unfortunately I didn't have anyone else to turn things over to but this incompetent son of mine.'

'Go to the demons, all of you,' grunted Montreico as he spilt his seed into the priestess' womb, his buttocks clenched and quivering.

The priestess was lying inert. She hadn't opened her eyes the whole time and Allura was scared she was dead. Apparently Montreico was too, because he was trying to rouse her.

'Look at me, bitch, acknowledge your new master.'

The priestess stirred slightly and her eyes opened, as she reached for the baron's throat. Allura thought the grasp would be feeble, but as she squeezed Montreico began to gasp for air. 'No,' the priestess countered, employing a voice not her own, 'you look at me.'

Her eyes were red as fire, the voice a low growl, sharpened by raw cruelty. Her body shimmered and Allura saw the priestess now as she had in the great hall when first the baron stripped her naked. Montreico was trying to pull himself free but she was holding him fast. Cries of distress came from the back of his throat, scarcely human, indecipherable in their fear and panic. Allura shielded her eyes against the visions, the accumulated pain being unleashed upon the man; the compounded suffering that had taken place in the dungeon, year after year, a huge psychic ball that the baron must now swallow.

Allura almost felt pity for him. He had his good side, and she had felt strongly for him at one time. But there were lines no mortal was allowed to cross. The shuddering of his body continued. Arcs of blue light passed between his cock and her invaded sex. He was being sucked dry of life, flames devouring his flesh. When at last the light faded there was nothing left upon the body of the priestess but shadowy wafts of smoke. Baron Montreico was no more.

'My son,' cried the dungeon keeper, 'where has he

gone?'

'Where he belongs,' said Saraveeta, rising to her feet.

Allura ran to the priestess. The woman lay as if dead, her wrists twisted over her head, her legs still wide like a rag doll.

'There is nothing you can do for her, Allura; there is nothing any of you can do,' said Saraveeta.

Allura watched as her old friend knelt over the inert redhead. Gently she caressed the priestess' cheek and brushed the hair from her face. 'Isn't she lovely?' Saraveeta whispered.

'Yes,' agreed Allura.

'One last kiss,' declared Saraveeta, 'and it will be done.'

'What will be done?' demanded Allura, tired of not knowing. 'What is happening? Are you really the princess? Have the gods spoken this to you?'

'The gods speak to all of us, Allura, if we listen.'

'I hear nothing. I never have.'

'It's all right, neither did I until I first laid eyes upon this dear woman. Now it all makes sense.'

'What does? Explain, Saraveeta.'

'Later. First the kiss; the kiss of sweet sleep, long deserved.'

'Yes,' murmured the red-haired priestess, her ruby lips dry and cracked.

Saraveeta wet her own and leaned closer, her sleek dark hair falling over the other female's face and mixing with her hair of copper. The touch of their lips was so sweet and desire filled, Allura felt the pull in her own body, their passion radiating outward, wiping over the princess like a warm wave, a blanket to cover her consciousness, a dream in physical form, wanting inside her, between her thighs and in her mind to bestow a gift unspeakable.

She could hardly keep her eyes open, and the next thing

she knew Saraveeta was above her, lifting her into her arms. 'The priestess,' Allura whispered.

'She is dead,' smiled Saraveeta, 'and I have taken her place.'

A thousand questions raced through Allura's mind, but she was in no position to ask even one. 'Hold me,' she said to her friend. 'Hold me tight.'

Chapter Nine

The Grand Duke Fortragian entered the hall to the sound of trumpets. It was much as the time before save that the old baron was now gone. In his place, to greet him, was the former baron, the onetime keeper of the dungeon, muchly scrubbed and richly garbed, though still unshaven.

'Baron Alexo,' the grand duke clasped his hand, the grip of both men strong and vigorous, 'we had assumed you dead.'

'I preferred it that way; as you know the pressures of nobility can become a bit overwhelming at times.'

'Of course.' He turned to Allura who was dressed in white, her hair coiled upon her head. She wore the crown of a princess, though more than likely she would be yielding it in just a few moments. 'My niece, you are more lovely than ever.'

'Thank you, uncle.' She curtsied humbly, mindful that she was already more slave than free.

'The great lady shall attend us presently?' the grand duke asked. They referred, of course, not to the old priestess but to the new one, she who had been Saraveeta, mere mortal, mere slave.

'Indeed.' The old baron frowned. 'As you know, we are here by her command. I myself had no wish to leave my dark home.'

'Yes, Alexo, I do marvel at that, how a man can grow accustomed to the absence of light, to the dampness and to the perpetual misery.'

'It was at times a bit bothersome,' he confessed, 'but where else than in a dungeon – that most delicious place of captivity and isolation – can one exercise such full and perfect power over a female? They are such marvelous creatures to be explored, my friend, so resilient and strong and yet so vulnerable. One may break them again and again finding ever lower levels of degradation. Their suffering redeemed me. I was blessed to feel and know their pain, and to bathe in their tears. This one's included.'

Allura lowered her eyes at the man's reference to her three days in his charge. It shamed her to hear such talk in front of her uncle, but the say was no longer hers. It had already been established that she was not the real princess. The augers had been taken three times, each time pointing to Saraveeta. On top of this a slave had been found, a servant of Saraveeta's family from many years ago who had confirmed the entire story, down to the last detail.

The queen had died giving birth to Saraveeta. The switch was made in dead of night, with much weeping on the part of Allura's natural parents, but under pain of sword they were forbidden to reveal the secret to anyone. Over the years they came to love their new child just as well, though it pained them no end to see Saraveeta so mistreated by the false princess. This was, Allura suspected, in part the reason they had left the kingdom, leaving behind no inheritance.

Which meant that Allura had nothing for her legacy but her own crime of harlotry – harlotry to a man who could no longer redeem her. Slavery was her only option, and being a slut, according to her uncle – who continued to call her niece only out of kindness – had cost her the right to an honorable death, the other possible sentence. Already the former princess would have been on some auction block, save that Saraveeta had ordered her appearance in this place, in the company of the ladies and lords of the realm.

'Yes, I understand; Montreico sentenced her to time in the dungeon,' said the grand duke, as though she were not in the room.

'Though my miserable killjoy of a son sent her down with the iron belt,' the old man lamented. 'Still, we had fun, didn't we?'

Allura nodded, unable to speak.

'When this is over,' the old baron whispered in her ear, 'I am going to feed my cock deep into your mouth.'

She felt the familiar flood between her legs, even as the grand duke excused himself to go and speak with another of his old friends. 'I fear he heard you,' lamented Allura.

The baron pinched her buttock, with all the practiced cruelty of a veteran torturer. 'What of it? You won't have any secrets for long. And don't think you'll hide that pretty cunt this time. I intend to thoroughly invade it.'

She tried to squirm away from the grip of the man, a full two inches shorter than her and thinner by twenty pounds. Where was her power now, her ability to egg him on and outdo his sadism with her own masochism? 'Please, baron, not here.'

'It's harder up here, isn't it? When you have a name and station.' He grabbed a nipple through her dress. 'Hard when people know who you are. Downstairs a different part of us takes over. The beast part, but it links to something higher, too, doesn't it? That's what makes us humans the go betweens, halfway between animal and god.'

Allura winced. With desperate eyes she saw that all were seeing and pretending not to, her uncle included. Her rational mind told her all this must happen. She would be enslaved, for all to see, but still a part of her clung to her pride.

'I want to hear you beg, Allura. Tell me you want it. Beg me to fuck you, right here on the floor.'

'I... I do,' she cried. 'I beg to be fucked on the floor.'

He grinned, the years falling from his face. 'And you will be... slave.'

Allura's spine chilled at the words. Was he serious? Her discomfort made the man grin all the more. 'And soon,' he added for emphasis. 'Very soon.'

The image of herself so subjugated and violated in front of all these highborn people would stick in her brain, flooding her consciousness even as the arrival of Saraveeta was announced. That she was the new intentionary priestess, the great mother seer, could not be argued by her entrance. She wore a gown of silver that made her face glow. Her hair was dressed up like the wings of a perfect raven born to fly only in the pure skies of the gods. Her eyes were lit with a power, far more than human.

There was no explaining the manner of her having been chosen for the job. It may have been ordained from the start of time or more recently engineered by the gods. The old high priestess had come here to save the kingdom from Montreico, perhaps knowing she would die in the process. Then again, maybe it was a kind of suicide or natural death intended to allow Saraveeta to take her place at this exact moment in time. To that end, Montreico himself may have been a pawn all along. The ways of the gods were truly mysterious, as were the ways and identities of their servants.

'She is breathtaking,' breathed Fortragian.

'Let's hope she's less explosive than the last one,' muttered the baron.

Fortragian and the other men bowed deeply at her

approach, making the holy sign of obeisance upon their chests. Allura, as a slave, knelt at her feet, though this woman had been her bedmate only a few hours before, showing her such mutual delight as she had never thought possible between two human beings.

'Baron, I thank you for your hospitality, your house is indeed grand,' said the priestess, as though she had not already been living here with her former mistress.

'And unfortunately you are making me see far more of it than I wish,' he replied.

The priestess smiled, not at all put off by his impudence. 'I assure you that was a temporary arrangement. We shall have you below ground before you know it.'

'I could take that two ways, priestess.'

She laughed, not the laugh of Saraveeta of old, but a deep, rich timbre. She was clearly changing, minute by minute now. 'You are an honest man, Alexo, and you have no fear within you. Do you know how rare that is? You are what the gods treasure most, above silver and even gold.'

'I doubt old Zuranos would put anything above his wenches, but I appreciate the sentiment.'

'Baron, may I be allowed to take the high place upon the dais?' she enquired.

'Be my guest,' he bowed.

The priestess inclined her head, thanked him and strode to the place Montreico had so zealously, even insanely guarded.

'I thank all of you,' she said when comfortably seated. 'You are all most gracious. I do apologize for the rather sensational nature of recent events, and for the suspense you must feel today. I promise all will make sense quickly. First, know that indeed I am the daughter of the king, hidden at birth to protect my life, the king acting under divine orders. There were those at the time who sought the life of the future priestess, hoping to end our line, but those persons long ago failed. So too has a more recent conspirator who hoped to use the person of the princess for his own ends.

'This is all to great good, however, as a result of hiding me and switching me with another baby, there have arisen great confusions not easily remedied. Allura, my oldest and dearest friend, will you step forward.'

Allura rose to present herself before the priestess.

'Allura, once princess and always my friend, you have my deepest sympathies for all that has befallen you. Had I known before I would have intervened for you. But I myself did not know who I was until the former priestess came and spoke to us in this very room. One look at her and I knew my true origins. Not only as a royal person, but as a future priestess myself. It became clear to me she was of my kind and that for whatever reason the gods had placed the next in line to her office in the birthing womb of a queen, destined to die in childbirth. The next high priestess after me may be a peasant, even a whore. We cannot say. The gods use us as they will, and the gods are always to be praised and feared. Still, as a mortal myself, Allura, I feel deeply for you.

'More than this, I am pledged to rescue your station and restore to you what has been taken away. Grand Duke Fortragian, will you approach me?'

The man did so, offering a stiff military bow.

'First to you, grand duke, I bring the thanks of the gods for the honorable, diligent and selfless exercise of office you have shown. The spirits of your ancestors are well pleased.'

He bowed again, clicking his heels crisply. 'May I both live and die in service, great lady.'

'Indeed, your place in the annals is assured and well deserved. In fact, I am of a mind to expand your station further and make you king.'

The duke's face turned ashen. 'But priestess, begging all forgiveness, I have no wish for this, nor am I equipped. I am far too old and I have no heirs.'

'But you could marry, could you not? Perhaps to this young woman here, whom we now know is no blood of yours or the king's. In this way the once Princess Allura will be what she should be: Queen Allura.'

'But priestess,' cried the duke, 'she has been as a niece, even a daughter to me, it would never seem right to my eyes.'

'But it is the will of the gods. It fulfills the prophecy left by the former priestess. An issue of this house is to be king. That issue will be the child of you and the baroness Allura.'

Allura knelt once more and put her forehead to the floor. 'Great lady, my uncle is right, this cannot be moral,' she protested, the sudden shock making her bold.

Saraveeta stood. 'That which is moral is what the gods decree. Frankly, I had expected better of you all. Show a little more gratitude, if you please. You may consider this interview at an end. Baron Alexo, will you prepare my carriage. I will leave at once. Feel free to crawl back into any hole you wish after that. You have my full blessing.'

The priestess walked imperiously past him, not waiting for an answer as she exited the chamber.

Allura and Fortragian looked white as ghosts, but Alexo started to chuckle. 'Maybe things aren't so boring up here in the sunlight after all, eh? Sorry about not being able to fuck you, Allura, but it seems you've slipped the noose of slavery yet again. We'll have to take a rain check. And Fortragian, all I can tell you is best find some eel root to keep that dick of yours hard – you're going to need it to produce that litter of fine strapping sons.'

'This can't be,' moaned Allura.

'The gods are cruel.' Fortragian clenched his fists. 'The gods do as they will.'

'No,' Allura vowed, 'this can't be and I won't let it.'

'Find a way to stop it,' snorted Alexo. 'You'd as easily rope a cloud or piss yourself an ocean.'

The words hit Allura like a bolt of lightning. It was true; she could not stop it. But there was one who could. It was simple, beautiful, almost absurdly easy. 'Thank you, yes,' she replied, 'I will.'

And with that she was running. Running from the audience hall of the baron to the small temple of stone wherein she'd been married; the temple wherein she'd lost her virginity. It was there she would pray and seek the direct intervention of Zuranos himself.

For if indeed the gods were the highest moral law as the new priestess said, then couldn't they remake it as they willed? Especially if they had a good reason. And in Zuranos' case that reason could and would be sex.

Bolting the door behind her, removing her shoes, she faced the altar. She must steel herself, step by step in her approach, and with each press of her bare feet upon the marble she uttered a fresh prayer.

'Hear me, great lord. Accept me. Do not turn me away, for I am yours and yours alone.'

Reaching the great stone slab she fell to her knees. For a long time she felt and heard nothing. It had always been this way for her. She had often wondered at temple services, watching others, if they had real experiences or if they merely pretended for the sake of being pious. She was wasting her time, surely, just as she had as a child when she'd come to pray for some particular thing or other she wanted.

'I never ignored your prayers. It is simply that they were unworthy. You prayed for no one but yourself and you'd already given more than you needed.'

Allura gasped. 'Who said that?'

'Who do you think?'

She leaped to her feet and looked about. She saw no one. 'Is it one of the priests?'

The voice laughed. 'I have no need of those old fools to speak for me. I prefer my priestesses. Ever so much more delicious to possess, don't you think?'

She knew now who this was, though it did not seem possible, not in reality. 'Father Zuranos, you are real.'

'Am I?' The god sounded amused. 'It is good to know this. I'm ever so grateful to hear it from the lips of such a fair maiden.'

'I meant no disrespect.'

'Actually it was blasphemy, but don't worry. I rather enjoy hearing my name in vain, contrary to what the priests say about me. Makes me feel all the more alive. You know really, your baron was more a man after my own heart than any of my so-called holy men.'

'Lord, I do not seek to understand your ways, only to make my entreaty. My cause is just.'

'By the blade of Sythos,' he boomed, his voice suddenly taking on the timbre of a thunderstorm. 'And what do you know of justice, you whelp of a girl?'

Allura fell instinctively to her knees, cowering. The room was filled with light and there appeared before her a silver-bearded man in a loincloth, his body robust and strong, like a squire of fifty who is accustomed to hard labor. He wore about his head a laurel wreath, one of his traditional symbols of power. Allura was overwhelmed at the sight of him; he was so beautiful and utterly desirable as a man.

At the same time she was filled with terror, for this was the king of the gods, the spinner of planets. In his eyes she could see it all, the depthless blue of the sea, the faraway light of the bluest star.

'Now this is a fine form.' He flexed his biceps as though the body were a mere suit he was trying on. 'Rather too long since I've used it, I think.'

Zuranos took a step forward, relishing every little motion, and as he approached Allura she shuffled back on her knees.

'Child,' he chided, 'why do you fear me? Am I not the father of you and all your kind? Do I not love you all?'

Allura thought of what the priestess had said about him taking the form of a bull-man, or a snake with a three-foot tongue for whipping. 'Yes, Lord Zuranos, we are grateful to you and we praise your holy name.'

'Nonsense,' he scoffed. 'You are a race of hypocrites and opportunists. I made you in my own image, I should know. And don't think for a minute I'm pleased by flattery. It bores me to tears.'

'It seems that the priests have misled us,' Allura noted.

'That's their job. Without a bit of guilt and fear all would do as they pleased and there'd be no end to the messes I'd have to fix.' He lifted her chin between thumb and forefinger, his touch warming her belly and tickling her nipples instantly. 'My, but you are a little beauty, aren't you? It never fails to amaze me how you creatures are put together, so sweetly, and so differently from your male counterparts.'

His aura was more than she could bear, and her original purpose now mixed with new needs; complicated, female needs. 'I seek to please you, Lord Zuranos.'

He arched a brow, sending a dark chill down her spine. 'Indeed? Brave words, don't you think?'

It was true. Allura had no idea what she was saying, and her only hope was to plead for mercy. 'Lord Zuranos, I come on behalf of my kingdom... the priestess has decreed to us that—'

'I know all about that.' He put a finger to her lips. 'You have been ordained to sire a child by Fortragian, to take him as husband, yet you refuse, thereby defying my will.'

The finger stilled her lips. It was as an instrument of discipline which, well wielded, seemed capable of bringing her much agony. Desperately she beheld him, continuing her plea with eyes alone.

'Fear not, little one, I care not if you thwart me, or hate me even. The question is what will you bargain with?' The divine finger circled her lips, making her draw short breaths. The tingle and the heat were making her limbs heavy with desire, and at his merest utterance she would open herself to him fully.

'My lord I offer myself,' she rasped, the words pouring from her like wine into a glass.

He toyed with her golden locks. 'If you mean your body, it is not yours to give. I am your creator. I possess you as I will.'

He brushed the rim of her ear, sending spasms all the way down to the lips of her sex. 'Yes...' she shuddered, 'you possess.'

'You know, my beauty, that if I enter you, you will be changed.'

'I understand,' she breathed.

'No you do not, but you will learn.'

'Yes, my lord.'

'It is not only your body but your mind I will take.'

She did not doubt it. She did not doubt he would delve deep into her subconscious, even into her dreams.

'Close your eyes, sweet Allura. Close them tight.' With

both hands clasping hers, the god drew her to her feet. His size dwarfed her, as did his bodily power. Beckoning her onto tiptoes he bestowed a kiss, hot as a brand, full and deep, reworking already her identity to his mold. She did not dare open her eyes against his will. As she stood, encircled in his embrace – a grip strong enough to hold the earth together or shatter a mountain – she felt the overwhelming tenderness of a flower petal, beckoning her into deepest sleep. Waking sleep, standing sleep, something ever so much deeper than anything manageable by mortals on their own.

The kiss seemed to last a thousand years. She was flying, watching her own body below as she soared overhead. The god was a bird, holding her in its clutches, ferrying her across the river dividing the land of men and that of gods. It was a sky river as well as a watery one, and they climbed and climbed and climbed until at last they were at the top of creation.

It was there that the bird let go of her and sent her crashing down through the miles of sky, down through the layers of reality. Down to her death.

Chapter Ten

'Careful, don't damage it; that'd be the fourth today,' grumbled an accented voice, something worthy of a lower class miner or ditch digger.

'Well there wouldn't be that many damaged if you'd leave me to my business,' complained a second voice.

Allura realized what these men were doing was extracting souls from a river, and hers was the one they were discussing. A net of some kind bore up underneath her – though she had no physical form – and she was lifted to the surface. The water was brackish, and even without a nose she knew it stank.

'Well, have you gotten it yet?' called a new voice, impatiently, and Allura's bare soul cringed to recognize it as Baron Montreico.

'Yes, master, we've got it right here.'

'Fetch it, then, and we'll fit it with a body.'

She didn't exactly feel it when they moved her, although she was aware of being on dry land.

'We've got some nice ones today, guv'nor,' quipped yet another new voice. 'Nice and newly patched together.'

'I want a prostitute,' he said. 'A big breasted slut with a slack cunt; we'll humiliate her from the get go.'

'I've just the ticket,' he chortled. 'Right this way.'

The voices grew a bit garbled, but she heard the baron say, 'No, don't bother with the stitching, just stuff it in.'

And right away Allura could open eyes again and grip her chest, which was indeed mammoth, with huge breasts, the nipples pierced with gold rings. She had a slight swell to her belly and her pussy was much looser, no doubt due to all the men who'd been inside her. Licking her lips she felt heavy paint upon them. Whoever this was, she'd died with her make-up on.

'How fetching you look, my bride.'

Allura turned her new head and saw the baron. He was much himself, save for the burns across his face and chest from his deathly encounter with the goddess.

'We saw you vaporized,' she said, though the point seemed moot under the circumstances.

'Bodies are preserved here from the exact moment of death, notwithstanding subsequent decay or destruction. Ordinarily people take back their own, but I thought it would be amusing to offer you a little change.'

Allura looked into the mirror he was holding. She was looking at a prematurely aged tramp, a well fucked young bitch who had likely died in some back alley of what looked to be asphyxiation, judging by the circles around her throat. 'I am not supposed to be here.' She touched her throat, feeling the deep red grooves.

'Nobody ever is, sweetheart, but you get used to it. And cheer up, at least now we'll have each other.' He handed her a collar, affixed to a leash. 'Put this on and we'll get you acquainted with your new home.'

She put the leather circle around her throat, the situation still strangely surreal. 'Am I dreaming?' she wondered aloud.

'Only if you want to consider the whole of your life a dream.' Montreico yanked the leash. 'Come, bitch, let's take you for a walk.'

Allura stumbled behind, along the raised wooden dock on which stood many naked people, or rather unoccupied bodies. At the bottom of the steps was a thin layer of warm mud.

She took a second to look up. The air was reddish brown and had a distinct odor of sulfur. The sun hung low in the sky, but it was black in color and gave off no light. Whatever it was illuminating this strange landscape of distant craggy mountains, blood-red clouds and greeny-blue mud, it was coming from somewhere else.

He continued pulling her along. It was foggy now and soon the mud opened into a road with grass on either side, thick and purple. The trenched roadway, barely a yard wide, was ankle deep with a disgusting black substance and Allura had no idea why anyone would use it as opposed to the grass.

'You'll go on all fours from this point on.' The baron yanked down on the leash and Allura collapsed on hands and knees. The mud squished between her fingers and toes. From down here it was more green than black, and she could detect no odor.

'How does it feel, princess, being led like a dog in hell? That's what you are, you know, a slut dog for all eternity. And I get to watch over you. Once a day I'll fuck you and make you rue the day you were ever conceived – alive or dead.'

'Baron, I did nothing to deserve hell,' she lamented, scurrying as best she could.

'Not true. You defied the god. Anyway, what does it matter? We all come here. The lot of us humans. It's a closely guarded secret, as you can imagine.'

The road led them through a town, simple wooden homes on either side, the unusual thing being that the occupants were being attacked, each within their own walls by horned, goat-like creatures with sharp teeth.

The baron stopped them in front of a barn-like structure. 'Here we are,' he said. 'This is where it will happen every day, for all eternity. To begin with you must try to escape.'

'Montreico,' she implored, 'I've no wish to play your games.'

The baron pulled a leather riding crop from his belt. 'You've no choice, my dear. Now escape, damn you.'

He lashed out with the whip, slicing her back. Allura cowered but he kept closing in, so at last she did as he'd told her and rose to her feet, and she was halfway down the street when the large dog-like animal downed her. It pinned her to her back and continued to stare down at her, large globs of drool dribbling onto her face and breasts.

'This is a tessral, its body is wolf and its soul is that of a madman. Mostly when we play this game it will catch you. Sometimes it will fuck you, other times I will kill it and fuck you myself — such as now, for example.'

The baron drew his sword and ran the beast through, whereupon it yelped and ran away, presumably to die.

'On your belly, my little slut. Back to the barn with you, and you'll receive an extra heavy thrashing for trying to escape.'

Allura choked on the mud. Now it stank and its color was red from the rabid wolf-creature's blood. The same creature she would encounter every day for the rest of eternity, sometimes merely to be gored, other times to be violated.

There was a crowd around the barn when they arrived; pot-bellied men, holding their severed cocks in their hands, old woman with four or five breasts apiece and various human legged creatures with the heads of other beings.

'This one isn't for you.' The baron shooed them away. 'Not today.'

Once inside he opened his breeches, and out spilled a penis at least a foot long. 'Like it?' he grinned. 'One of the fringe benefits of afterlife.'

Allura watched as he took down the saddle, bridle and bit, placing them on the hay-covered floor.

'That's for after. For now, stick out your tits and we'll start with them.' He wielded the whip and Allura instinctively covered her large breasts, an action that only served to make the baron angry. 'You shouldn't have done that. Now I'll have to use the rats.'

He whistled, calling a pair of snow-white rodents with pink noses and long white teeth. They were smaller than she'd expected, more like mice.

'The beautiful thing about this,' said the baron, pulling Allura by the hair and tying it to a rope hanging from the ceiling, 'is that whatever damage they do is erased by sundown.'

Allura was on tiptoes, feeling like a human bell as she hung from her own hair. 'Hands down,' he warned, 'or I'll cut them off.' She couldn't avoid flailing as he raised the rats to her vulnerable breasts.

'Oh, for hell's sake,' he muttered. 'You're making this so complicated.' He uttered some sort of incantation and at once a spider appeared behind her, one large enough to pin back her arms using a pair of its legs.

'Now for a little narcotic,' he encouraged the terrible spider, and it sunk huge teeth into her neck and she felt a hot liquid being injected.

'That's a poison. A special one. It will paralyze you and lock you into a state of perpetual orgasm. Unfortunately, it also amplifies pain.'

The giant spider made a hissing noise as it finished its business, while the baron attached the rats to her nipples, and quite efficiently they clamped on as he let them dangle.

'Don't look down,' said the baron, introducing yet another element of terror, but Allura did and now there was no barn floor beneath her, only a cascading pit, a cradle of fire, the cauldron of the universe. From various cliffs and crags on the way down hung human souls, shadows of gray with clawed fingers slipping, clinging for life.

'One minute here can feel like a million years, Allura.' He stroked her forehead. 'How long has it been already? Your body looked the same when they brought it here, but I swear I've been away from you long enough for you to have aged a hundred years.'

There was sadness in his eyes and self-pity, an emotion she now understood to be the lifeblood of this place. 'You will never keep me, baron,' she vowed.

His lips curled into an arrogant smile. 'Oh, won't I?'

Once, twice she blinked in her excruciating pain, and now it was he who was the tessral, the madman cloaked as a dog. With a snarl in place of intelligible speech it leaped upon her, thrusting her back against the wall. Teeth, cock and claws sunk in and it fucked her, the sexual death clutch, designed to kill a victim in seconds.

Allura screamed and then she was a scream herself. Then again she rose within the sound and felt herself lifted aloft on some kind of wind – a wind that should not be.

A reprieve that should not be.

'Why should I let you past me?' said the sentinel at the gate, and Allura beheld the creature of black obsidian, half bird, and half lion, winged and clawed, its eyes plucked from an ancient king and dipped in liquid emerald.

Where was she? Was she alive again, or could it be the baron had lied to her about there being only one place for the souls of the dead?

'Because,' said the fleeing Allura, back in her own body, golden hair streaming behind her, 'I can pay my passage.'

She did not know how she knew to say that. It was like in a dream, when speech comes to you of its own accord, knitted by laws of reason that do not hold when awake.

She also knew her time was short. At her heels nipped and snarled the tessral. She'd been given this opportunity, one time only and she must not waste it.

The sentinel held the creature at bay with an ominous point of its claws. 'With what coinage will you pay?'

'The universal coin,' she replied, 'of female to male.'

She floated to him, hands at her sides. The penis of the sentinel was enormous and as she approached it grew and grew, bigger than her own body, and instead of ingesting it as she'd intended, she found herself absorbed into the hole at the end. The sentinel sighed with the sensation. It must have been a very long time for him. Luxuriating herself in the soft pink expanse of his tube, she did the miraculous work of pleasuring him from within.

'You can't get away with this,' the baron was calling from outside the tunnel.

But it was too late for him. The sentinel's heart was beating; his flesh was pulsing around her, enveloping Allura in male desire and male satisfaction. The testosterone filled her lungs. Her every pore was bathed in its sensual powers. She responded in kind, locking her body into a fetal position, out of which she was going to squeeze her own orgasm, in time with his.

'Yes, yes,' came the voice of the sentinel, encouraging her, and Allura needed no more prompting. Clutching her breasts and sex she rocked her pelvis, bringing just the right friction to trip her clitoris.

They both went off together, sliding down a precipice, like a mud fall at spring, down into a green valley, unoccupied and pastorally perfect. Allura felt herself spasming as they rolled over and over until finally she was on her back, in a field full of wild flowers representing every color of the rainbow. She was young again, barely eighteen, in a dress of light blue cotton. Porfino was above her, wanting to make love.

'It will feel so good,' he encouraged, trying to push up her dress.

'But this is wrong,' she said. 'If we get caught it will be my ruin.'

'What have I to lose?' he teased. 'You'll only have to marry me and I'll be king.'

'Not king,' she corrected. 'Only a prince.'

'Give me your hands,' said Porfino, and she held them out for tying.

'Now put them above your head.'

Again she did as he said, putting her bound and crossed wrists in a position of complete surrender.

'There, now you are my slave.'

Young Allura giggled. 'Don't talk like that, Porfino.'

'Why not, if I want to?'

'Because it's naughty, that's why.'

'But slavery is natural, for women, at any rate.' He fondled her golden hair, loose and free. 'I shall name you Goldie,' he decided, 'and you may thank your master for giving you a name.'

Her voice was thick with desire as she said, 'Thank you, master.'

Never had the real Porfino been so manly and never had anyone so quickly taken her in hand. This was another dream; that explained it.

'Your name is a gift, slave, I may take it away at will.'

'Yes, master.'

His fingers ran over her breasts. 'I own these.'

'Yes,' she agreed, 'master.'

'And I own this.' His hand crept under the dress, between her thighs. 'Spread your legs wider, Goldie, give your master access to his cunt.'

Allura moaned as he dominated her perfectly, and ruthlessly.

'Come, Goldie, come like a little slut on my hand.'

The dirty, demeaning talk and the pressure on her clit sent her into convulsions. She couldn't hold it back even if she wanted to.

'Now lick.' He held his come-soaked fingers to her mouth when she had ridden the tide of her bliss, and Allura lapped meekly, even her tongue exhausted.

'Good girl,' Porfino praised. 'I think you've earned some time with my cock now. What do you think?'

'Yes please, master,' she whispered, and Porfino – or whoever he really was – pulled down his loose breeches and mounted her face. She smelled deeply his balls, and then took the gift of his penis, pushed home between her lips.

'Take it all, Goldie, or it'll be the strap for your ass.'

Obediently she deep-throated the young man, sucking him determinedly.

'You're a natural cocksucker,' he observed, her head bobbing up and down. 'You should be made to perform in the public square, taking on every erect cock, naked on your knees. Or how about leaning over in the stocks? Then they could have your mouth and cunt, and your ass, too. Would you like that?'

Allura clenched her fists. She couldn't move her arms, and yet she needed so badly to cup her hand to her cunt and bring herself relief from the torrential heat of his words.

'I'm sure you would,' he answered for the cock-gagged slave. 'You're exactly the kind of slut to get off on something so disgusting.'

Porfino's rhythm grew faster and faster. His eyes were

ablaze and she braced herself for his release, the contents of his turgid cock spurting into the back of her throat. But clearly he intended more – more abuse for her, more pleasure for him.

Climbing off her, disengaging from her hot mouth, he ordered Allura onto all fours, naked in the field like an animal. He made her hand over her dress and the rest of her clothes, taunting her that perhaps she would get them back, or perhaps not.

'How does it feel, Goldie,' he wanted to know, 'to be naked and helpless before a man? Crawl,' he encouraged. 'Let me see your slave ass move.'

Allura padded on all fours, the tall grass brushing her cheeks. Tiny insects darted about her face and flitted over her back, but she could not remove them – she could not get up.

'If I wished I could leave you like this,' he mused, 'and you would have to find your way home. Someone would find you on the road, I suppose, and take you... home, that is.' There was no mistaking the pun; clearly there was another way she could be taken and that way would be sexually.

'We are going to end your virginity, Goldie. Are you wet for me?'

Allura knew that while the other questions were rhetorical, this was the one she must answer. 'Yes, my master, I am wet.'

'You will take me in a single thrust, like a good slut.'

'I will try, master.'

Porfino broadsided her ass with the side of his boot, sending her sprawling. 'You will do more than try, now get up slave girl.'

She resumed her position, a bit shaky, spitting grass from her lips.

'Now, will you be a good slut and take your master's cock in one thrust?'

'Yes, master, I will take your cock as you say.'

'On your elbows, slave girl. Head to the ground, ass in the air.'

Allura assumed the exquisitely vulnerable position, her cheek pressed to the grass.

'You have a very good ass, Goldie. It is difficult to say if I'd rather beat it or fuck it.' Porfino ran a hand across her, then inside her, obscenely. 'What do you think?'

'Master must do as master wills,' she reasoned.

'True enough, Goldie.' He dangled a finger over her clitoris, and then pulled it back, delivering a hard smack. 'Pain,' he said, 'and pleasure.'

Allura moaned, the barrier in her mind somewhat unclear. Thrice more he repeated the lesson till her senses were thoroughly confused. She was thrusting out her ass, craving the impact of his hand and cringing at the mild touch of his finger on her sex lips.

'Even your sensations,' Porfino concluded, 'are not your own.'

'Yes, master.' Her voice was a rising pant, lifting into the clear blue, make-believe sky.

'Shall I mount you now?'

'Oh, master, Goldie begs to be used.'

He rubbed her bottom then spanked her harshly. 'If I enter you, it will be in one thrust, and you will perform with perfection.'

'I will please you, master. I am your slut.'

'You may not come without permission,' he warned, his cock at the lips of her sex.

'No, master, I will not.' She shook her head determinedly. 'I will only obey, I will take your cock and I will please you.'

'Of course you will,' he condescended, 'you are my pet.'

The pet Allura groaned from the bottom of her soul as he fulfilled, at long last, his promise to breach her, his threat and declaration to end her virginity and begin the concrete expression of her slavery.

'Is that enjoyable?' he asked.

'Yes master, yes.' A thousand times yes, but still the question nagged. Who was he and where was she? Had she made it back across the river, through the gates out of the regions of hell, or was this some new bizarre torture? Had she really and truly lost her life? And where had Zuranos gone? He'd tricked her, it seemed, abandoned her, but why? Did he not want her for himself, at least for a little while before casting her away?

This much she knew: the cock fucking her was not Porfino's, nor was the body. Not that she could keep hers from responding. A cock is a cock, especially when one's virginity is being taken all over again and one is locked in a lovely fantasy of submission.

'Remember, not before I say,' he reminded.

Porfino's hands were on her hips. She could feel his cock expanding and she knew it was time. Strange, she felt none of the virgin's pain. The dream, it seemed, was flawed in its details.

'You are a most difficult creature, you know that?' the god complained. 'I suppose you critique my sunsets as well?'

Allura turned her head. 'Zuranos?' she gasped, but when she looked it was the baron's father, Alexo, fucking her.

'I told you,' the old man cackled, 'I'd have my chance.'

'No,' she squealed, 'I don't want to play this game anymore. Do you hear me, Zuranos, or whoever is in charge? I don't want to play.'

Alexo helped himself to her rectum. 'Gods' juices, that's good,' he grunted, sounding like a man about to expire. 'So sweet and tight. I believe you're even tighter than when you came to the dungeon.'

She tried to dislodge him from her, but he was not budging. Nor was he very likely to, now that he'd gotten hold of such a tasty little prize.

'Zuranos!' she cried. 'Help me!' At once the sky of pastoral blue began to darken, ominous clouds rolling. Without thunder or rain came streaks of silent lightning in deep orange, wizened fingers reaching between the earth and the heavens, and wherever it touched the grass or trees they were quietly consumed, everything in their path scorched to dust, but for the two of them.

In place of the old baron behind her and in her, however, she now saw the head of a snake, its body the thickness of a stout branch. She knew it at once to be Zuranos, and rising she began to run, Montreico's words loud in her ears.

You will be run down, the same each day, for all eternity.
It was like she'd never left the baron's hellish city after all, but was still there dreaming of escape. But had that city been real, or was that yet another trick? Was the god setting her up all along?

Laughter in the wind, swirling about her, confirmed her worst suspicions. She'd been in the hands of Zuranos all along, the god playing every part, from the baron to the sentinel to old Alexo. All were avatars, spirit made flesh.

'Good girl.' The god picked her up in hands of cloud. 'My sweet, sweet love.'

Allura felt the decay wash away, her soul cleansed of every experience he'd forced upon her. She was to be herself again, but first Zuranos would have her naked.

No flesh at all.

The god came to her in a room of white, his form that of a man garbed in gold, his hair of gold, his skin bronze, his eyes the color of burnished copper, his body chiseled, every muscle to perfection. He wore golden sandals and she was upon a bed of white, her skin as pure as alabaster. Golden cords held her limbs wide apart. She was helpless, and by her own will, too.

'Good girl,' repeated Zuranos in his new guise.

Allura looked into his eyes and recognized. 'Tesotoro?'

The god laughed and crawled upon her, his cock rigid. Sinking deep, like a sword, paring her unclothed soul, he sealed the union, a knowing beyond the world of mortals.

Images flashed through her mind, her life in bits and flashes, like cords whipping round. She reached to touch them, the filaments of cracking light, the balls of glowing knowledge. So many possibilities...

'Yes, my daughter,' the god encouraged, slowly moving in and out of her. 'The greater gift I give to you.'

Greater than what? She had no voice with which to ask.

'I am coming,' said Zuranos, and the world was born again. Old stitches pulled from the fabric, new ones added. The hand of Hechira, queen of gods, mixed with those of the king. A new cloth, its pattern leading all the way up to the life of a young princess.

Back, back in time she was swept, to a time before it all began.

Allura had been having a nightmare. Her father was being killed all over again before her eyes and a man was standing by, laughing. He called himself a baron and he had come to claim her soul – and her hand in marriage. Her great uncle had been powerless to stop it happening. For the wedding she'd been tied to a chair, a gag in her mouth.

Saraveeta was forcing her down the aisle, whipping her all the way.

Awaking in a cold sweat Allura sat bolt upright. 'Veeta!' she cried. 'I need you!'

The slave, who had been sleeping beside her on the floor, hurried to her side. 'Mistress, what is happening?'

'I had a horrible dream. Tell me, what happened yesterday?'

Veeta cocked her head. 'Yesterday? Why, you had another suitor, a count named Raysar. From the east.'

'Yes,' she enthused, 'it's coming back to me. I thoroughly humiliated him. I told him to fuck you, didn't I?'

The slave girl lowered her head, her black hair hanging about her face. 'Yes, mistress.'

It really had all been just a dream.

'So you are really still my slave?'

'W-why wouldn't I be, mistress?' the girl asked nervously, guarded against some sort of a trick.

'Pinch your nipples then, as hard as you can.' She needed to test her powers, and naked Veeta squeezed obediently with thumb and forefinger, increasing the pressure until at last she winced, exhaling against the pain, but she did not stop until Allura allowed her to.

'Oh, Veeta,' she cried, 'I'm so happy! You wouldn't believe how terrible it was. A baron took me away and threw me in a dungeon, preferring you. Then the priestess herself came. Can you imagine it? There was a terrible battle and then you were the priestess. You said I had to marry my own uncle because he wasn't really my uncle. You were the real princess too, and I had to pray to Zuranos for help, and then… oh, never mind, it wasn't real. Go and draw a bath, Veeta, I want to cleanse myself of the memory.'

'Yes, mistress, I will do so at once,' the slave said obligingly, hurrying to do the princess' bidding. What a pathetic little creature she was. To think she could ever have been the real princess.

Allura continued to gloat and enjoy her reprieve all morning, until at last she was notified of the day's list of suitors. There were three; two being minor nobles with utterly boring names, but the third caught her attention.

'The name is here, but no accounting of his status,' she said, pondering the short list. 'Who is this Tesotoro?'

The vizier cleared his throat. 'He isn't actually a noble, highness,' he offered, somewhat sheepishly.

'Who is he then?'

'He is…' the man hesitated uncomfortably, 'a warrior. By his own account called to come here to seek you out. The grand duke had originally ordered him thrown out, but he comes under seal of the priestess.'

'The priestess?' Allura felt a strange chill. The priestess of the dream? And why did this name Tesotoro seem familiar? 'Whose priestess?' she asked cautiously.

'The Great Mother Seer, of course,' the man stated. 'Who can refuse any who comes under her banner? Though obviously you can never marry a commoner.'

'No, obviously, but I would see him, and see him first, before the others. Immediately, in fact. Send him to me.'

The vizier bowed. 'As you wish, princess.'

'I have seen you,' said Allura, as soon as the man appeared.

The tall blond with broad, bronzed shoulders and sturdy frame, his hair braided down his back, regarded her. 'Have you?' he mused confidently. 'I cannot imagine where.'

'Would you believe I dreamed of you?' she said, feeling strangely nervous. 'Though you were different then. You worked for a baron, by the name of Montreico.'

'I know of no Baron Montreico.'

She tried to place the accent. 'You are not from our kingdom.'

'I'm barbarian,' he said proudly. 'From a land where the hair of all is glorious yellow, like yours.'

Allura blushed. 'My hair is not at issue; your intrusion here is.'

His hands were at his sword belt. He wore a shirt of mail and heavy leather trousers tucked into riding boots of dark brown calfskin. 'This is no intrusion,' he said simply. 'I was sent by the god.'

'Many claim divine inspiration for many purposes; why should I believe you?' she asked skeptically.

The barbarian ignored the question, but looking about the room he asked, 'Where is the girl, Saraveeta?'

Allura tensed. 'How do you know of her?'

'Why does that matter? I would see her, is all.'

Uncertainly the princess called for the slave, who was scrubbing her bathing quarters. She looked fetching, her skimpy brown rag of a dress soaked, her face smeared with cleansing powder.

'Yes, mistress?' She knelt at once, putting her head to Allura's feet.

'This one should not be a slave,' said Tesotoro. 'You have done her great injustice.'

Allura fumed. 'How dare you judge me?' she snapped. 'Get out this instant or I shall have you thrown in the dungeons.'

'Yes, that's another specialty of yours,' he said derisively.

'You do not know me,' she said defensively, quite fearful that he did. 'And whoever has fed you these lies will hang from the gallows by morning.'

Tesotoro seemed quite unimpressed by the outburst. 'You will free her,' he said simply, 'at once.'

'I will do no such thing!' She laughed contemptuously, but with little conviction. 'In fact, I shall have your freedom too, just as I have hers.'

The warrior removed his gloves. 'This is your last warning,' he vowed.

'What are you going to do,' she scoffed, 'strike me?'

'Strike you as an enemy male, no, but I shall strike you as a spoilt female; over my knee.'

Allura retreated to her desk, grabbing an ivory letter opener. 'Approach one step and I shall cut out your heart,' she threatened. 'Veeta, run and call for help.'

'No,' said Tesotoro to the girl, 'stay where you are.'

Veeta looked back and forth, eyes flitting between her mistress and the new man. She seemed unsure whom to obey.

'Do as I say, or I'll have your head,' Allura warned.

'Saraveeta,' Tesotoro countered calmly, 'go to the bath chamber and wash yourself. Your serving days are over.'

Saraveeta hesitated a moment longer, took one last look at Allura, and scurried for the bathroom.

'Bastard,' the princess cursed, arcing a slap at his face, but the large man easily swayed back out of range and caught her swinging wrist in one brawny fist, instantly spinning her around and pinning her arm up behind her back.

'You are badly in need of learning some respect,' he informed her.

'Perhaps,' she panted, continuing to struggle, 'but not from scum like you.'

With contemptuous ease the warrior pushed her across to the nearest chair, and sitting down he laid her across his lap, just as he'd promised. With a flip of her skirts he bared her underclothing, and with one hand pressing on her back he used the other to insolently caress her buttocks.

'You will die for this!' she cursed, but Tesotoro merely delivered a punishing blow, her rage instantly reduced to girlish protests.

'That hurt, you animal!' she complained. 'You can't do this to me!'

'Oh, but I can and I will.' Thrice more he smacked her, his seasoned palm cracking upon her soft behind. Allura moaned, wriggling against him, terrified that her reactions were turning sexual. This was a beautiful man and she wanted him inside her, all the more so for his masterful treatment of her. 'Are you prepared to behave?'

'No,' she answered honestly.

'Then we will continue,' he said calmly, and Allura was spanked into submission; in a matter of minutes he had her begging to be able to obey him and do his will, even to free Saraveeta from slavery.

'Get up,' he told her at last, and the princess stood, legs shaking, her bottom throbbing and her cheeks glistening with tears. 'That is how a female is handled,' he told her. 'Whether she be crown princess or a lowly whore, all respond alike to discipline. All need it, as well.'

Allura made no response.

'Now, call Saraveeta,' he ordered, and she did.

'Do not kneel,' said Tesotoro to the slave, his eyes moving sternly to Allura. 'The princess has something to say to you.'

Allura lowered her eyes, feeling like a chastised child. 'I was wrong to enslave you, Saraveeta,' she said, so quietly the other two in the room barely heard her, 'and I give you back your freedom.'

Saraveeta's eyes widened in shock. 'It is true,' confirmed Tesotoro. 'The princess has had a change of heart. She has seen the wickedness of her ways.'

'Mistress?' Saraveeta enquired, looking for final confirmation.

'Get out of here, damn it,' Allura snapped. 'Do you want to gloat forever? Don't you think this is hard enough for me already?'

'Sorry mistress,' the girl babbled excitedly, and then left hurriedly.

'You are a spoilt little girl,' Tesotoro said when they were alone. 'But fortunately for you most men find that attractive to a point. Gives them more control in the end. And now,' he rose to his feet, 'I'll be going.'

'But you said you came for me.' Suddenly Allura did not want him to go. 'Isn't that what you told my uncle?'

'I merely said the god delivered me to see you.' He shrugged. 'And I have done that, for the purpose of freeing Saraveeta.'

'Why?' she asked. 'What's so special about her?'

'She is to be the next priestess,' said Tesotoro. 'I am to escort her back to the temple, and there she will live the remainder of her days.'

Allura's knees almost buckled. 'The dream,' she whispered.

'The dream?' he echoed. 'What dream?'

'Nothing,' she shook her head, 'it is nothing.'

The warrior left her without so much as a goodbye, and for a long time she stood there, trying to absorb what was happening. Pieces of her nightmare were coming true – the appearance of the blond barbarian, and the part about Saraveeta being elevated to the rank of priestess. Was there more in store for her?

Her thoughts turned to fleeing, but where would she go? She knew no one outside the castle. It was tempting to run to her uncle, but he was an old man and could no longer give her the protection she needed.

If only her father were alive. He would have handled things and none of this would have happened. There were the gods to pray to, but she had a growing suspicion that prayers had already gotten her in a good deal more trouble than she could handle. What if Zuranos were playing with her mind?

Tesotoro. She must go to him. He could explain things. He came from her dream, but he lived here and now. Besides, Allura was flushed and very aroused and she needed to know how a mere commoner could do that to her, and without showing any finesse or gentleness.

She found him in a guest room provided by the vizier. His plan was to rest for the day, taking Saraveeta back to the temple the next morning. He was in only his breeches, chest bared, lying upon the narrow bed. 'Yes?' he said impatiently, not having bothered to get up to answer her timid knock at the door.

'Tesotoro,' she demanded, 'who are you really?'

He regarded her, unperturbed. 'I am the first man to spank you. It has an effect, doesn't it?'

'Not a pleasant one,' she sulked. 'Especially not when the man in question has come to life from a dream.'

'Yes,' he admitted, 'and I have dreamed of you, too.'

'Y-you have?' she gasped, her cheeks coloring.

'Indeed, princess.' His eyes smoldered. 'I have dreamed of you naked in my bed, obeying my commands, serving my every whim.'

She swallowed hard. 'That would be impossible.'

'Not really,' he shrugged. 'I could break you in one night. It is only that I do not care to.'

'And why is that?' she probed, trying not to sound interested.

'Because then I will have to marry you, and I don't want the responsibilities of rule on my shoulders.'

Allura ran a hand softly over her tingling stomach. 'You could always denounce me for harlotry, instead,' she offered, her voice a breathless whisper.

'I suppose I could,' he considered, 'but I doubt you would enjoy life with me much.'

'Why not, Tesotoro?'

'Because I am used to whores and slaves,' he told her frankly. 'I have no patience for ladies.'

'Maybe I don't want to be a lady.' The princess lifted her dress over her head.

'Beware,' said Tesotoro, 'you are only reacting to your spanking. Quite soon the passion will wear off and you will hate me.'

She pulled off her undergarments, baring herself. 'But that moment is not now.'

'You are a virgin,' he stated.

'Perhaps not for much longer.'

'I might be tired,' he teased.

'Perhaps I can revive you,' she countered mischievously.

'Leave me.' He rolled to one side, his back to her, but Allura crept onto the bed like a tigress.

'Must I beg you?' she asked, and he allowed her to briefly nibble his earlobe.

'Woman, this is your last chance,' he said.

'Last chance at what?' she asked playfully, and when her hand crept around to his crotch he finally moved into action.

'All right,' he grumbled, 'you've asked for it now,' and Allura quickly found herself beneath him, pressed beneath toned muscle and smooth skin, the scent of the male filling the air.

'Will you be gentle?' she asked softly.

'I will be as a man. No more, no less.' She sighed, melting beneath him. 'I won't let you go,' he breathed against her throat. 'Not after this.'

'No,' she clutched his shoulders, 'please don't.'

'It will be forever.'

'I'll count on it,' she hooked her legs around his firm buttocks, 'I am yours.'

'Consider yourself taken.'

Indeed, she did. Taken, and given, and redeemed. The only question that remained was where her dream had come from and what role the god had played.

'Maybe this world is the dream,' teased an inner voice, 'and the other was real.'

'Does it matter?' she replied, as she and Tesotoro melted together.

'No,' said the voice of Zuranos, voice of creation and of every spirit and every possibility, 'it does not... so long as I get my share of you.'

Allura shivered, thinking of the many nights ahead. With Tesotoro and the god both. In a way she was lucky; it wasn't every woman who got to cheat on her husband with the lord of the universe.

More exciting titles available from Chimera

1-901388-09-3*	Net Asset	*Pope*
1-901388-18-2*	Hall of Infamy	*Virosa*
1-901388-21-2*	Dr Casswell's Student	*Fisher*
1-901388-28-X*	Assignment for Alison	*Pope*
1-901388-39-5*	Susie Learns the Hard Way	*Quine*
1-901388-41-7*	Bride of the Revolution	*Amber*
1-901388-44-1*	Vesta – Painworld	*Pope*
1-901388-45-X*	The Slaves of New York	*Hughes*
1-901388-46-8*	Rough Justice	*Hastings*
1-901388-47-6*	Perfect Slave Abroad	*Bell*
1-901388-48-4*	Whip Hands	*Hazel*
1-901388-50-6*	Slave of Darkness	*Lewis*
1-901388-51-4*	Savage Bonds	*Beaufort*
1-901388-52-2*	Darkest Fantasies	*Raines*
1-901388-53-0*	Wages of Sin	*Benedict*
1-901388-55-7*	Slave to Cabal	*McLachlan*
1-901388-56-5*	Susie Follows Orders	*Quine*
1-901388-57-3*	Forbidden Fantasies	*Gerrard*
1-901388-58-1*	Chain Reaction	*Pope*
1-901388-61-1*	Moonspawn	*McLachlan*
1-901388-59-X*	The Bridle Path	*Eden*
1-901388-65-4*	The Collector	*Steel*
1-901388-66-2*	Prisoners of Passion	*Dere*
1-901388-67-0*	Sweet Submission	*Anderssen*
1-901388-69-7*	Rachael's Training	*Ward*
1-901388-71-9*	Learning to Crawl	*Argus*
1-901388-36-0*	Out of Her Depth	*Challis*
1-901388-68-9*	Moonslave	*McLachlan*
1-901388-72-7*	Nordic Bound	*Morgan*
1-901388-80-8*	Cauldron of Fear	*Pope*
1-901388-77-8*	The Piano Teacher	*Elliot*
1-901388-25-5*	Afghan Bound	*Morgan*
1-901388-76-X*	Sinful Seduction	*Benedict*
1-901388-70-0*	Babala's Correction	*Amber*
1-901388-06-9*	Schooling Sylvia	*Beaufort*
1-901388-78-6*	Thorns	*Scott*
1-901388-79-4*	Indecent Intent	*Amber*
1-903931-00-2*	Thorsday Night	*Pita*
1-903931-01-0*	Teena Thyme	*Pope*
1-903931-02-9*	Servants of the Cane	*Ashton*
1-903931-03-7*	Forever Chained	*Beaufort*

ISBN	Title	Author
1-903931-04-5*	Captured by Charybdis	*McLachlan*
1-903931-05-3*	In Service	*Challis*
1-903931-06-1*	Bridled Lust	*Pope*
1-903931-08-8*	Dr Casswell's Plaything	*Fisher*
1-903931-09-6*	The Carrot and the Stick	*Vanner*
1-903931-10-X*	Westbury	*Rawlings*
1-903931-11-8*	The Devil's Surrogate	*Pope*
1-903931-12-6*	School for Nurses	*Ellis*
1-903931-13-4*	A Desirable Property	*Dere*
1-903931-14-2*	The Nightclub	*Morley*
1-903931-15-0*	Thyme II Thyme	*Pope*
1-903931-16-9*	Miami Bound	*Morgan*
1-903931-17-7*	The Confessional	*Darke*
1-903931-18-5*	Arena of Shame	*Benedict*
1-903931-19-3*	Eternal Bondage	*Pita*
1-903931-20-7*	Enslaved by Charybdis	*McLachlan*
1-903931-21-5*	Ruth Restrained	*Antarakis*
1-903931-22-3*	Bound Over	*Shannon*
1-903931-23-1*	The Games Master	*Ashton*
1-903931-24-X	The Martinet	*Valentine*
1-903931-25-8	The Innocent	*Argus*
1-903931-26-6	Memoirs of a Courtesan	*Beaufort*
1-903931-27-4	Alice – Promise of Heaven. Promise of Hell	*Surreal*
1-903931-28-2	Beyond Charybdis	*McLachlan*
1-903931-29-0	To Her Master Born	*Pita*
1-903931-30-4	The Diaries of Syra Bond	*Bond*
1-903931-31-2	Back in Service	*Challis*
1-903931-32-0	Teena – A House of Ill Repute	*Pope*
1-903931-33-9	Bouquet of Bamboo	*Steel*
1-903931-34-7	Susie Goes to the Devil	*Quine*
1-903931-35-5	The Greek Virgin	*Darke*
1-903931-36-3	Carnival of Dreams	*Scott*
1-903931-37-1	Elizabeth's Education	*Carpenter*
1-903931-38-X	Punishment for Poppy	*Ortiz*
1-903931-39-8	Kissing Velvet	*Cage*
1-903931-40-1	Submission Therapy	*Cundell*
1-903931-41-1	Caralissa's Conquest	*Gabriel*
1-903931-42-8	Journey into Slavery	*Neville*
1-903931-43-6	Oubliette	*McLachlan*
1-903931-44-3	School Reunion	*Aspen*
1-903931-45-2	Owned and Owner	*Jacob*
1-903931-46-0	Under a Stern Reign	*Wilde*

ISBN	Title	Author
1-901388-15-8	Captivation	Fisher
1-903931-47-9	Alice – Shadows of Perdition	Surreal
1-903931-50-9	Obliged to Bend	Bradbury
1-903931-48-7**	Fantasies of a Young Submissive	Young
1-903931-51-7	Ruby and the Beast	Ashton
1-903931-52-5	Maggie and the Master	Fisher
1-903931-53-3	Strictly Discipline	Beaufort
1-903931-54-1	Puritan Passions	Benedict
1-903931-55-X	Susan Submits	Heath
1-903931-49-5	Damsels in Distress	Virosa
1-903931-56-8	Slaves of Elysium	Antony
1-903931-57-6	To Disappear	Rostova
1-903931-58-4	BloodLust Chronicles – Faith	Ashton
1-901388-31-X	A Kept Woman	Grayson
1-903931-59-2	Flail of the Pharaoh	Challis
1-903931-63-0	Instilling Obedience	Gordon
1-901388-23-9	Latin Submission	Barton
1-901388-22-0	Annabelle	Aire
1-903931-60-6	BloodLust Chronicles – Hope	Ashton
1-903931-62-2	Angel Faces, Demon Minds	Rael
1-901388-62-X	Ruled by the Rod	Rawlings
1-903931-67-3	A Cruel Passing of Innocence	Jensen
1-901388-63-8	Of Pain & Delight	Stone
1-903931-61-4	BloodLust Chronicles – Charity	Ashton
1-901388-49-2	Rectory of Correction	Virosa
1-901388-75-1	Lucy	Culber
1-903931-68-1	Maid to Serve	Gordon
1-903931-64-9	Jennifer Rising	Del Monico
1-901388-75-1	Out of Control	Miller
1-903931-65-7	Dream Captive	Gabriel
1-901388-19-0	Destroying Angel	Hastings
1-903931-66-5	Suffering the Consequences	Stern
1-901388-13-1	All for her Master	O'Connor
1-903931-70-3	Flesh & Blood	Argus
1-901388-20-4	The Instruction of Olivia	Allen
1-903931-69-X	Fate's Victim	Beaufort
1-901388-11-5	Space Captive	Hughes
1-903931-71-1	The Bottom Line	Savage
1-901388-00-X	Sweet Punishment	Jameson
1-903931-75-4	Alice – Lost Soul	Surreal
1-901388-12-3	Sold into Service	Tanner
1-901388-01-8	Olivia and the Dulcinites	Allen

All **Chimera** titles are available from your local bookshop or newsagent, or direct from our mail order department. Please send your order with your credit card details, a cheque or postal order (made payable to *Chimera Publishing Ltd*) to: **Chimera Publishing Ltd., Readers' Services, PO Box 152, Waterlooville, Hants, PO8 9FS**. Or call our **24 hour telephone/fax credit card hotline: +44 (0)23 92 646062** (Visa, Mastercard, Switch, JCB and Solo only).

UK & BFPO - Aimed delivery within three working days.
- A delivery charge of £3.00.
- An item charge of £0.20 per item, up to a maximum of five items.

For example, a customer ordering two items for delivery within the UK will be charged £3.00 delivery + £0.40 items charge, totalling a delivery charge of £3.40. The maximum delivery cost for a UK customer is £4.00. Therefore if you order more than five items for delivery within the UK you will not be charged more than a total of £4.00 for delivery.

Western Europe - Aimed delivery within five to ten working days.
- A delivery charge of £3.00.
- An item charge of £1.25 per item.

For example, a customer ordering two items for delivery to W. Europe, will be charged £3.00 delivery + £2.50 items charge, totalling a delivery charge of £5.50.

USA - Aimed delivery within twelve to fifteen working days.
- A delivery charge of £3.00.
- An item charge of £2.00 per item.

For example, a customer ordering two items for delivery to the USA, will be charged £3.00 delivery + £4.00 item charge, totalling a delivery charge of £7.00.

Rest of the World - Aimed delivery within fifteen to twenty-two working days.
- A delivery charge of £3.00.
- An item charge of £2.75 per item.

For example, a customer ordering two items for delivery to the ROW, will be charged £3.00 delivery + £5.50 item charge, totalling a delivery charge of £8.50.

For a copy of our free catalogue please write to

**Chimera Publishing Ltd
Readers' Services
PO Box 152
Waterlooville
Hants
PO8 9FS**

or e-mail us at
info@chimerabooks.co.uk

or purchase from our range of superbly erotic titles at
www.chimerabooks.co.uk

*Titles £5.99. **£7.99. **All others £6.99**

The full range of our wonderfully erotic titles are now available as downloadable e-books at our website

www.chimerabooks.co.uk

Chimera Publishing Ltd
PO Box 152
Waterlooville
Hants
PO8 9FS

www.chimerabooks.co.uk
info@chimerabooks.co.uk
www.chimera-connections.com

***

Sales and Distribution in the USA and Canada

Client Distribution Services, Inc
193 Edwards Drive
Jackson
TN 38301
USA

***

Sales and Distribution in Australia

Dennis Jones & Associates Pty Ltd
19a Michellan Ct
Bayswater
Victoria
Australia 3153

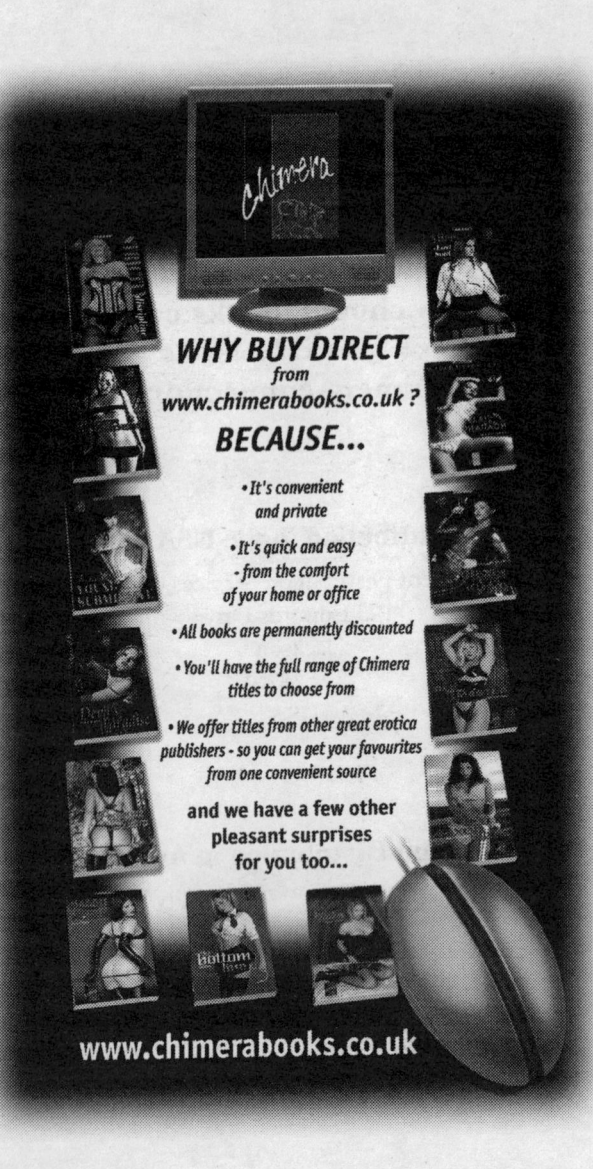

WHY BUY DIRECT
from
www.chimerabooks.co.uk ?

BECAUSE...

• It's convenient
and private

• It's quick and easy
- from the comfort
of your home or office

• All books are permanently discounted

• You'll have the full range of Chimera
titles to choose from

• We offer titles from other great erotica
publishers - so you can get your favourites
from one convenient source

and we have a few other
pleasant surprises
for you too...

www.chimerabooks.co.uk

Chimera
WANT TO
MEET
SOMEONE
SPECIAL?
Whether you're
interested in
finding romance,
or perhaps some
adult fun,
we can help.
Go Online at...
www.chimera-connections.com